T0197137

An Etruscan

Spring

An Etruscan
Spring

~ *April in Paris* ~

Lorna J. Shaw

authorHOUSE®

AuthorHouse™
1663 Liberty Drive
Bloomington, IN 47403
www.authorhouse.com
Phone: 1 (800) 839-8640

Published by AuthorHouse 09/09/2015

ISBN: 978-1-5049-2687-4 (sc)
ISBN: 978-1-5049-2686-7 (hc)
ISBN: 978-1-5049-2688-1 (e)

Library of Congress Control Number: 2015912929

Print information available on the last page.

I wish to dedicate these books to my two daughters,
Karen Shaw Dhir, and Frances Shaw Vinskas, who,
by their patient devotion made what, would have been
an intolerable journey, a blessing in disguise.

An Etruscan Spring

fumum et opes streptique Romae
The smoke and wealth and din of Rome
Horace: Odes: circa 62 BC

Chapter One

Douglas Parker sat at a table in an outdoor cafe in the Piazza di Spagna. He sipped his cappuccino and watched a swarthy workman wrestle a huge azalea bush into an old wooden barrow and wipe his hands on his leather apron. Now he was in Rome, in a cosmopolitan metropolis completely foreign to everything he had ever seen and every place he had been in his sixty years. *Was it only four days ago that they had left behind the heat and dust and odours of Kenya? Four days since they bade goodbye to Michael and Dorian and Julianne? Four days since, they had arrived in Rome with its noise* and traffic congestion and odours, heavenly odours of pasta sauces, sausage and garlic, and *bread baking in ovens at the rear of shops?* He glanced at his watch and wondered how much longer Margaret would take to complete her shopping, all those gifts for the family and a few friends back home. He drained his cup and drew a guidebook from his pocket.

They had arrived in Rome at sunset. By the time they had cleared customs, night had settled over the Eternal City. The taxi had deposited them at the Columbus Hotel on the Via del Conciliazone, an imposing edifice of at least fifty years, quite new by Roman standards. The shabby baroque furniture in the lobby and their room bespoke of other, kinder days.

Margaret had perched on the bed and gazed up at the intricate moldings around the high ceiling. The room seemed cold in character as well as temperature and she reached over to touch the radiator below the window. It was stone cold.

"It isn't the Ritz, is it," Doug murmured as he came out of the bathroom drying his hands on a towel.

"No. But what do you expect for a quarter of a million lira?"

They had rested the following morning, and after a leisurely breakfast in the hotel dining room, they had made two decisions: to find a restaurant with a more reasonable fare, and to take a bus tour of the city that afternoon.

The bus, in fact was a van, large enough to accommodate six people as well as a driver and tour guide. Two German couples who spoke no English had settled into the front seats. "This is great," Doug muttered as Renaldo, the tour guide, had pointed out various landmarks along the way, most of the time in German, because it took too long to repeat the information in English. The van driver, Michel, had sped up the Via del Conziliazone toward the Vatican City, careened right with such alacrity that Doug whispered "I bet this fellow's descended from a charioteer."

Margaret had smiled grimly. "I hope we get out of here alive!"

The tour had led north into an elegant residential area and paused at a point in Monte Mario to look south and eastward across a dusky panorama of domes and rooftops, St. Peter's Basilica, the Vittorio Emanuel monument, the Coliseum and glimpses of the winding course of the Tiber River. The van had descended through green avenues of cypress to cross the river and made a wide circuitous route through the Borghese Park. Doug consulted his guidebook and said quietly to Margaret, "This was once a malarial swamp. Some fellow named Hawthorne described it as a place where `fevers walk arm in arm and death awaits'."

Margaret looked at the page. "Hawthorne ... I think he was an American, a novelist ... Well, it isn't a swamp now... Look.... There's a family having a picnic."

The van had entered a busy street and they learned that they were now about to enter the old city through Porto del Popola, 'the gate of the people, the route of conquerors and kings', Renaldo explained. Because the traffic had grown considerably, their guide now had time to repeat himself in English, and he pointed out the features of the huge piazza, the obelisk, the fountains, as Michel had forced an entry into the melee of cars, trucks, bicycles, scooters and pedestrians on the Via del Corso. White-gloved policemen stood at the intersections to enforce the system of traffic lights amid honking horns. They shouted Italian obscenities at recalcitrant drivers emphasizing the words with white-fingered gestures. By the time they had traversed the Piazza Venezia and viewed the Vittorio Emanuel monument which Roman citizenry dubbed "the typewriter" or "the wedding cake" because of its garish facade, Doug was chuckling. He leaned toward Margaret and said, "I like this Hawthorne's sense of humour. When he saw this place he bemoaned the sight and sighed `Even the ruins are ruined'!"

Renaldo was now pointing south to the Coliseum. After another hair-raising escape from a collision, Michel had stopped at the entrance and Renaldo led his white-faced group through one of many arches into the arena. As Doug listened to the German explanation he looked about and decided that here, before him stood a perfect ruin. Some of it was still intact. They climbed several rows of seats to gain a perspective of the many ringed tiers, once, accommodating thousands upon thousands of spectators. The floor had disappeared, but below stood the supporting pillars and evidence of the cells where the hapless gladiators or prisoners had awaited their fate. Margaret took his arm and shivered as the shadows fell across the crumbling walls. "You can almost hear the cries, the clamour.."

Renaldo came alongside. "A huge building, yes? Everything else is small. The engineers, the builders, they make a perfect job. They even make a canvas covering to shield the crowd from the sun." He pointed toward the centre of the arena. "And they make a wooden floor so tight to flood with water so they can enact sea battles with ships."

Doug raised his eyebrows. "Really!"

Renaldo nodded. "Yes, but mostly we remember this place for the fights. Here, men were thrown to the lions in the morning, and to the bloodthirsty crowd in the afternoon. The gladiators … Their combats ended in death. The emperor chose but it was the roar of the crowd that made him turn his thumb to the ground …"

Doug nodded. "Two thousand years have passed but the gruesome history remains."

Margaret asked. "How many Christians were murdered here? … And does their blood still cry out for vengeance?"

Renaldo stared at her briefly and said, "Many years ago, the church sanctified this ground because of the blood of the martyrs." He turned and clapped his hands. "Shall we go on?"

Michel was waiting to take them on beyond the Baths of Caracalla where they had turned onto the narrow Appian Way and jolted very slowly over the ancient stones, the road where Caesars' armies marched toward the sea and set forth to conquer distant peoples.

They came to the catacombs. Renaldo had herded them toward a yawning stairway and they had descended into a labyrinth of tunnels and shafts where the bones of saints had once been interred. Many of these bones now, reposed in museums, and below the altars of churches and cathedrals. Margaret plucked Doug's sleeve in the dim light and confining space. "I'll wait for you at the top of the stairs," she said, and fled.

He came to her some time later and they returned to the city along a broad thoroughfare. "Well, that was interesting," he said. "Interesting but gruesome, skulls and bones, but they have to use their imaginations to identify the saints. No one kept dental records then." The bus slowed momentarily as the traffic increased.

"The site of the Circus Maximus," Renaldo had said as they whizzed past an empty field.

His tour group stared with glazed eyes at the long green mound where in former days a quarter million Romans gathered to watch the chariot races. Crowded narrow streets delayed their return to the hotel and the sun was setting beyond the dome of St Peter's at the end of the street before they said goodbye to their companions and paid Renaldo and Michel a generous tip.

Doug took off his shoes and stretched out on the bed. "I think we can do as well with the guidebook, as paying those fellows for their services."

Margaret turned on the water in the bathtub and came back into the room. "I think so too. Let's try it tomorrow by ourselves."

A cold drizzle in the morning changed their plans and they had taken a cab to the Vatican Museums instead. Unprepared for the immensity of the exhibits, they bravely bought the five hour itinerary that would guide them through almost five miles of display.

"We'll never see everything," Margaret said.

"We can try," Doug replied and led her by the hand into the Egyptian gallery.

Four long hours later, they came to the Sistine Chapel and waited in line to enter. An overwhelming collection of sculptures, paintings, tapestries tumbled in their minds. The immortal works of art had been breathtakingly beautiful. "Wasn't the Laocoon unbelievable?" Doug said remembering the sculpture of giant serpents slaying the Trojan priest and his sons.

"Yes," Margaret replied. "There was such strength, such anguish … And I never realized that marble could look so much like skin. I almost thought the Apollo would draw a breath."

"The Etruscan Museum was good too," Doug said. "I understand that the museum in Tarquinia is even better though."

"I'm changing my mind about museums," Margaret said. "I had no idea they could be so fascinating."

He smiled. "So I'm a good influence on your cultural leanings."

She smiled at him. "I guess so. Of course, these are exceptionally good museums, the finest in the world. But take the library here for instance. It's not at all what I imagined. I thought it would be gloomy and full of books. But instead we found a beautiful bright hall with vaulted colourful ceilings and walls. And there in glass topped tables were manuscripts from the middle ages, Henry Tudor's petitions for annulment of his marriage to Catherine of Aragon; Mary, Queen of Scots' lacy hand requesting justice and her final pleas for mercy."

The queue had moved slowly into the Sistine Chapel, now restored after almost five hundred years of accumulated grime. The wait was worth it to gaze upon the kaleidoscope of colour overhead and on the walls. The vibrant scenes of creation and judgment overwhelmed them with the intensity of the drama, the history of man, his fall, his redemption, unfolding before their eyes.

Doug rubbed the back of his neck. "I ache just from looking at it. Poor Michelangelo. It says that he worked here `in great toil and weariness of body. I have no friends and don't want any. I haven't time to eat.'

"The agony and the ecstasy," Margaret mused. "His genius must have been a torment but think of the rapture of giving life to this concept. Just look at how a bearded God reaches down and stretches his finger to Adam."

"And yet he never considered himself to be an artist. He always signed his work named Michelangelo, sculptor only! And consider his physical pain too, working here day after day, head bent back, arms outstretched, paint spattering his beard and eyes. It says he was desperate to quit the commission but the Pope Julius would not allow it. He endured four years of forced labour but what a gift he gave to the world!"

Leaving the museum they had crossed the street to a trattoria. Crowded, because of the inclement weather, the restaurant was warm and noisy. Margaret sipped her steaming tea. "I wonder where I have been all my life," she said. "I realize I know so very little about what has happened in the world. And the artists who have left their work for us to see today … I couldn't have imagined anything like this in my wildest dreams … The talent, the genius of these people. The Laocoon must be over two thousand years old … It's too much to grasp with one's mind, isn't it."

Doug swallowed another piece of his panzerotti. "The chef who made this is a genius too. It's a work of art."

She laughed. "Are you tired to go to St. Peter's today?"

He shook his head. "Not if we take a cab."

The obelisk and fountains were barely visible across the teeming piazza as Margaret and Doug hurried through the colonnade, ignoring the outstretched hands of derelicts who sought shelter from the rain. The Swiss Guard had also taken refuge elsewhere and there was no one to protect the tourists from the beggars and gypsy children who found the Bernini promenade an adequate location to secure funds.

Climbing the broad steps to enter the basilica, they stopped suddenly, awestruck by the opulent interior of the old building. The massive pillars, the colossal cherubs, the brilliant gold statuary overwhelmed them. The monumental dome soared high overhead, supported by four huge twisted pillars. A bronze canopy hovered far above the papal altar in the center of the building. Guidebook in hand, Doug steered toward a chapel on the right and they beheld another of Michelangelo's creations, the Pieta. Margaret stared at it with a critical eye. "Jesus looks so small, wasted, emaciated … I always thought he would have been much more, more robust. And his mother looks so young … I don't know whether I like this …"

Doug frowned. "You have to remember, dear, that Michelangelo didn't copy this sculpture from a snapshot. And maybe he didn't have a bigger piece of marble …"

She shrugged. "I know I'm being silly. And it is beautiful. Look at the veins in Jesus' arm, and the hole in his hand. It is truly amazing when you look at it closely …"

They ambled across the tiled floor, heads tilted backwards to see the soaring columns, the golden window above the altar, a bronze throne and above it a wood and ivory chair purported to have belonged to St. Peter. The bronze statue of the old saint watched over the worshippers, the toes on one of his feet worn to a nub by the fervent kisses of the faithful pilgrims for centuries.

They had descended into the grotto and tombs below the papal altar. The excavations had extended beneath the foundations of the basilica built during the reign of Constantine in the fourth century. More treasures, priceless chalices were on view in the sacristy.

They ascended by elevator to the base of the dome for a view of the church. Margaret declined to climb to the top of the dome on a claustrophobic stairway so Doug went on alone to view the panoramic view of the Vatican Gardens and the city. "The rain's stopped," he said on his return "and the view was spectacular."

Wearied from the previous day at the Vatican, they had slept late and then taken a cab to the Piazza di Spagna for brunch. Doug had trailed Margaret through the shops before returning to the piazza while she chose from the selections of silk and woolen scarves. Her shopping now complete, she touched his shoulder. "How was the cappuccino?"

He rose to help her settle the bags on an opposite chair and signaled the waiter for service. They sat contentedly through the late afternoon watching the tourists mingle with the people who worked in the offices about the square. "I read that this place used to be unsafe after dark."

She raised her eyebrows. "Used to be? Isn't it still?"

"There's not much of a problem now. I understand the government has really cracked down on the gypsies and the petty thieves. No. It says that once upon a time, if a fellow walked through here after dark, alone, he stood a very good chance of being shanghaied into the Spanish navy, never to be heard from again."

Margaret stood up. "Let's go. I want to climb the Spanish Steps before dark."

Returning to their hotel, they walked along the square through aisles of vendors of roasting chestnuts, and Ethiopians on the Pont D'Angelo selling fake Gucci bags, carved elephants and plastic GI Joes. Levantine centurions posed outside the Coliseum with gleaming daggers poised at the throats of Japanese tourists. Amputees and stooped beggars extended brown palms in the shadows of the ornate, gold-encrusted basilicas and shrines. Gypsies played violins on the subway while their women carried sickly babies and tin cups; myriads of T-shirt venders, postcard hustlers and merchants of alabaster Davids, Pietas, and discus throwers, all conducting business amid the fumes of diesel engines, speeding scooters, honking car horns, police sirens and the wail of the ubiquitous ambulances. Sighing, Margaret said, "Nathaniel Hawthorne was right. Even the ruins are ruined! Oh dear. Now I'm getting a sore throat.'"

The Parkers had found respite in the winding shadowy alleys which opened suddenly onto bright piazzas with splashing fountains and red geraniums and yellow marigolds dancing in the sunlight; the little sidewalk restaurants with steaming cappuccino and heavenly scents of baking bread in the panificio near their hotel.

Margaret sneezed as Doug emerged from the bathroom with a towel in his hands. "Is your cold getting worse? Have you got a fever?"

She sat up. "No. I think I'm just overtired. An aspirin or two and a couple of days rest and I should be fine."

Doug sat down on the edge of the bed. "Would you like to cut all this tourist stuff for a while and go up the coast to Tarquinia? The Etruscan museum in the Vatican has whetted my appetite for more of their artifacts. We could check into our hotel at the beach and you could rest while I tramp around Tuscany for a day or two."

Margaret nodded. "Would you mind? We haven't begun to see everything here in Rome."

"Rome isn't going to go away for a while. It's been around for two and a half millenia so we can wait a few more weeks to see the rest of it." He reached for the telephone and then changed his mind. "I'd better go down to the desk to make arrangements. I speak Italian better with my hands than my mouth."

Chapter Two

THEY ARRIVED IN a rental car at the Tarquinia Lido the following afternoon after a harrowing drive north on the auto strada and checked into a small hotel in a stand of umbrella pines about a block from the rolling breakers of the Mediterranean Sea. Glass paneled doors opened onto a sunny balcony on the second floor and Margaret sank onto a chaise. "Just leave me here. I think I'm in heaven."

She spent the next two days reading, dozing and basking in the spring sun while Doug prowled the museum and tombs in Tarquinia and returned each afternoon to report on his activities. She tried to appear interested but her mind lay elsewhere, in the hospital wards of Beyanatha where little hands reached for comforting arms.

"Do you feel well enough to travel tomorrow?" Doug asked as he came to sit on the balcony with her.

She raised her eyebrows.

"I met an archaeologist this afternoon, a Brit ... Philip Longfellow ...He's investigating another necropolis. It's up near Volterra."

She summoned an unfamiliar enthusiasm and replied, "Yes. I'd like to get out and about. It's time I find out what happened to the Etruscans."

Returning from the trattoria that evening amid a downpour of pine needles, they heard the waves crashing on the beach. "It looks like we're in for a storm," Doug remarked. "Perhaps we won't be able to go tomorrow after all."

A heavy driving rain thrashed the windows late into the night and a grey drizzle the next morning caused a postponement of their plans.

They spent most of the day indoors reading, dozing and watching the CNN newscasts on the small television set. "And I thought you were going to read me poetry," Doug said. "The sun isn't shining but that's okay, isn't it?"

Margaret smiled and reached into her bag for the small volume Sonnets from the Portuguese. "I wondered if you'd remember?"

Waves lapped the shore the next morning and bright sunlight permeated the damp chill of the pine forest outside their windows. Philip Longfellow drove into the parking lot and came into the small dining room to join them at breakfast. A tall, youthful, balding man with a crooked smile and blue eyes, dressed in a tweed jacket, beige cashmere turtleneck and jeans. He proved to be an amusing chap and a knowledgeable companion on Etruscan antiquities. He pleaded a complete lack of any poetic talent, and ignorance of any connection to Henry Wadsworth Longfellow. Margaret laughed aloud when he said, "I think my family name originated in the Dark Ages because my ancestors had large feet."

They set off into the bright morning across the brown undulating hills of Tuscany, leaving the busy thoroughfares behind and drove slowly through villages where the farmers lived and worked the surrounding fields. Olive orchards and vineyards stretched upwards and gave way to scrub pine and cypress on the precipitous inclines bordering deep ravines. As they drove north, Philip pointed to various features of the landscape. "We're coming to Vulci. This was probably the most important seat of the Etruscans' bronze industry. They got the copper ore from Mount Amiata, about thirty miles up this river."

From the back seat, Margaret gazed down at a black stream.

"It probably wasn't fully navigable even then," Philip explained. "There is evidence that they built some roadways along its course."

Doug shook his head. "The industry of these primitive people … It's amazing to think that almost three thousand years ago they were able to do this."

"They weren't all that primitive, Doug. When we get farther up the coast I'll show you a place, Populonia, where they smelted iron ore from Elba and the islands. It was a tremendous industry for the time, so much so, that the Phoenicians and Mycenaeans began trading with them and they opened up a huge market. The warring Mediterranean people wanted all the iron the Etruscans could produce and the Etruscans became very wealthy shoppers. In fact, most of the urns and vases we find in their tombs came from Greece. When Mussolini began to build his war machines he used the slag from the Etruscans' operations to reclaim the iron they weren't able to refine."

They stopped several times that morning to look at the scenery and westward toward slits of pale limestone across the deep blue sea, little islands, inhabited by tourist hotels amid tangled olive trees and cacti. Populonia was a busy shipping port with ferries to Elba and Sardinia. Its crowded markets on precipitous streets proved a diversion to the men and Margaret followed them through a poor museum. "The problem in Italy," Philip explained as they exited the dusty premises, "is that there's very little money to take care of the antiquities. There's such a demand for the present, all the social problems that abound, education, health care … Someone aptly said `Our children hold us hostage. They are our commitment to the future'."

Doug glanced at Margaret and looked at his watch. "Well, they're right. And I think I'm committed to having lunch." He glanced at his feet and said, "These black socks look horrible with my track shoes. I couldn't find the mate to my brown one this morning."

They found a quiet piazza on a side street leading out of the city and enjoyed a substantial meal in the shade of a huge beech tree. Tempted to linger over a second cup of coffee, Philip pushed his chair back from the table and said, "No afternoon siestas now. On to Volterra."

They drove up winding mountainous roads and crossed high Apennine meadows where sheep grazed on the scrub grass. The car would then plunge down inclines into dark glens of fern and limestone. Philip had to shift gears to make the final grade up to Volterra which perched on a lofty hill surrounded by an alabaster precipice. They skirted the business section of the town and stopped for a moment to view the Porta Dell`Arco, an ancient gate to an even older city. Leaving Volterra's outskirts the car crept down another steep incline to a winding road through a long valley. Philip finally turned into a grassy area where a small van was parked beside an arrow pointing to a path that disappeared in a tangle of brush and vines bordering another steep wooded hill.

"Well, here we are," he announced. "I suggest we walk on the road up to the top of the hill and cut across the field. It's easier to reach the site from above. The path is pretty steep and hard to manage at times. I'll get my knapsack out of the boot and we'll be off."

While he was engaged, a group of young people emerged from the pathway laughing and talking. Doug and Margaret smiled at them. "Was it worth the climb?" Doug asked.

They stared at him and one said, "Non comprenez."

Philip closed the boot and spoke briefly to the French teen-agers. He slung the bag over his shoulder and started to walk toward the road. "They weren't at the site," he explained as Doug and Margaret drew alongside. "They were looking for pot … marijuana. Someone told them it grows wild up here."

"Does it?" Doug asked.

"I think it may. I know the police keep an eye on the place, checking who's coming and going …"

Margaret decided by the time they reached the top of the hill that this was the last hill she would climb today. Her cold had improved, but with the altitude and the exertion, she was breathing heavily and wondering if she should have remained on the chaise at Tarquinia instead. Turning off the road, she stumbled behind the two adventurers across a huge plowed field. "I'll be lucky if I don't sprain my ankle," she muttered and struggled to keep up to the two men whose long legs were more adept at crossing the deep furrows.

Philip stopped to rest and picked up a fragment of pottery. "We call this landscape archaeology," he said. "Teams of students go out to walk the fields and discover what the plows have turned up. We find everything from the prehistoric to the modern … clusters of bricks, shards, mosaics. All of the dating is based on pottery.

It's really a shame the ploughs go so deep now. Too many of the artifacts are fragmented." He tossed the shard away. "When you visit the necropolis at Cerveteri or Norchia you'll see the pottery that was discovered earlier. In the springtime, the earth seems to grow potshards."

They came at last to a clearing on the edge of an embankment and a spectacular view of a deep gorge and a purple mountain range on the eastern horizon. A dog barked as it spotted the intruders and a thin column of smoke curled from the distant chimney of an old house beside the field. "Here we are," Philip said. "This is the site of the town they've discovered. Watch your step now."

As they began their descent Doug reached for Margaret's hand and helped her over a series of rough steps leading to several muddy excavations on the side of the hill. Fenced by a perimeter of yellow tape the holes gaped at them. To one side, lay a swath of plastic sheeting covering a pile of plastic crates and some screens.

"I should have guessed no one would be working today," Philip said. "With all this rain … Anyway, let's go on down further and see what else they've found."

Margaret was growing weary and wondering why anyone in their right mind would spend their time digging in all this mud. "What have they already found?" she asked trying to appear interested.

"Last week, on the third level, they found a wonderful bronze mirror and an intact painted drinking cup and amphora. And before that, on the second level was jewelry … a gold earring carved with a woman's face, a brooch with an onyx inlay. The craftsmanship was exquisite. They're being examined now in the museum at Volterra. We think there may have been an attack on this town and these valuables were buried in haste. Only time will tell what really happened. We don't know how big this place was or who lived here or when? It'll take several years of digging to put the pieces together."

They managed to scramble down a few more ridges and found rows of stones which suggested the foundations of buildings. Margaret admitted to herself that even now, she could see some remnant of a civilized society, and as she roamed along a probable street, she came to what appeared to be an intersection and another street with excavations in evidence. Shrubs and low vegetation covered most of the area but she came upon several digs where the earth had been removed and she could see walled rooms. Doug and Phil crouched over a foundation examining a possible inscription. After Margaret watched them rubbing and wiping the stone with their handkerchiefs, she meandered along an ancient street and finally sat down on a low wall to contemplate the scene. *I wonder what it would be like to have lived here then ... Five, six or seven centuries before Christ ... What gods would I have worshipped? I read that God planted eternity in the human heart. Would I be searching for the one true God and the meaning of life? Or would I have even cared? I know of sins of greed and lust and pride. Would my heart be so deadened by sin that I would be consumed by getting material possessions, or finding a mate to meet my needs, or living wantonly using any man to further my ambitions ... Or would I be constantly dealing with the aftermath of wars with neighbouring states and trying to keep a family clothed and fed?*

"You're looking very serious, dear."

Doug's voice interrupted her thoughts and she looked up at him and smiled. "I was just thinking about what it would have been like to live here way back when...."

He reached for her hand. "See. You are learning to like history." He pulled her to her feet. "Come on. Phil says we should be on our way. He wants to take us to his friend's house in Siena for a cup of tea."

She brushed the twigs from her slacks. "That sounds like a great idea. I'm ready for a cuppa or is that what Australians say? What do the British call it?"

"I think they call it a cup of tea."

Phil called to them from the edge of the clearing. "Here's the path to the parking lot."

Suddenly, they heard a loud rumbling that seemed to come from earth below and they turned to each other with mouths agape and wonderment in their eyes. The ground beneath their feet began vibrating and they clung to each other to remain upright as a mighty roaring burst upon their ears like a freight train bearing down on them. Doug grabbed Margaret's hand and, screaming, they ran toward the excavations to escape the thundering forest. The earth trembled as they jumped into a hole and remained lying in a heap, as rocks emerged from the hillside and crashed to the bottom of the ravine. As the bowels of the earth continued to heave, they raised their heads and watched in horrible fascination as the green scenery moved slowly and majestically down the hill. They still clung to each other after the air around them grew still, listening to the sounds of trees cracking and snapping amid the echoing thunder at the bottom of the hill.

An eerie silence hung across the denuded hillside. Doug stood up and called, "Phil?"

Sensing his fear, Margaret scrambled to her feet. He turned and shouted, "Phil!"

Margaret covered her mouth. "Oh God!" she breathed.

Doug started forward. "Phil!"

"Don't go … It isn't safe …"

"I've got to find him. You stay here."

He left her clinging to a sapling beside the excavation and stepped carefully out on the barren hillside. His voice echoed across the valley. "Phil! Phil!"

He spied him about twenty feet below, wedged against a large rock, almost completely buried in earth and debris. Slipping and sliding down to Phil's side, Doug cleared away the dirt covering his head and was relieved to find his friend still breathing but unconscious. "I've found him. Come carefully …"

By the time she too, had slid down to the rock, Doug had uncovered more of Philip. She helped scoop the remaining debris from his body. The mottled colour of his face and hands alarmed them. His left leg was obviously broken with the foot turned away at an awkward angle. They stared at each other with stricken eyes. Blood seeped through the denim of his jeans."

"Look……. His….. leg must be broken very badly. He's so pale there must be bleeding somewhere else internally …"

"We mustn't move him …"

"No. And we'll have to go for help …"

"One of us will. We can't leave him here by himself …"

Margaret knelt beside Philip's head and opened his eyelid. "I don't know why I'm doing this," she said. "I don't know what to look for."

Doug cleared his throat again. "I'll have to go and get help for him. Will you be alright staying here by yourself for a while?"

She looked up at the barren hillside and said, "There's no trees left to fall down so I guess it will be okay."

A low moan startled them and they peered anxiously at Philip.

"Can you hear me?" Doug asked, kneeling down at his side. "Can you hear me, Phil?"

Another long moan.

"It's his leg… He's in pain … Perhaps we could twist it back into alignment … You know, put a splint on it, or something?"

"I haven't had a first-aid course in years," Doug sighed. "I'm not sure how to go about it … Let me think …"

"There might be some slats back up the hill where they were digging. We could use some of those fencing stakes."

"I'll go and see what I can find," Doug said, and with some difficulty, managed to scramble back up the hill.

Margaret remained kneeling beside Philip, contemplating their situation and thanking God that all three of them were not lying in a heap, broken and unconscious. Her knees were becoming very wet from the earth and she realized that Philip too must be growing cold from lying on the damp earth.. She rose and walked over to the edge of the clearing. "Doug?"

His voice floated down on the quiet air. "What's wrong?"

"Can you bring that plastic sheeting too? We need to cover him up, to keep him warm and dry …"

Several minutes lapsed before Doug appeared again half dragging a plastic bundle behind him. "I found some extra tape too," he said. "And you're right about keeping him warm. I think we should try to move him onto the plastic sheet if we can. He needs to be kept dry too."

He dumped the stakes and tape on the ground and spread the sheet beside Philip's body. "Now, if you can lift his feet at the same time as I lift his torso it should be okay."

"What if his neck is broken?"

Doug rubbed his chin. "Well, okay then, we'll forget about his feet and you hold his head steady while I lift him here."

Philip moaned again as they carefully lifted him onto the sheet and, once that was accomplished, they turned their attention to his long legs. Small patches of blood had leaked through the denim but there did not appear to be a significant haemorrhage so Doug left well enough alone and placed several stakes along the leg. Margaret bit her lip as he pulled and twisted Phil's foot into what looked like the normal position. Producing his jack knife from his pocket, he cut several lengths of tape and slit the leg of Phil's jeans to expose a nasty wound of white bone and bloody flesh below his knee. Then they managed to fashion a rough splint. Philip moaned several times throughout the procedure and Margaret said, "I think that's a good sign. At least he still has some feelings in his legs."

"I think I should try to cover the wound but we don't have anything, do we? Our handkerchiefs are pretty grubby... I can use my shirt" Doug stood up and took off his jacket and, unbuttoning his shirt, slipped it off his shoulders and used his knife to slit it and tear it into strips. The blade slipped and produced a long gash across his palm "Ow! Dammit! That hurt.!" Margaret fumbled in her shoulder bag and took a wrinkled tissue to dab the blood on his palm. She tore a strip off the shirt and wrapped his hand.

Doug opened Philip's knapsack and found a thick woolen cardigan. "This should help keep him warm," he said tucking it around Phil's torso.." I hate to leave you here, dear, but I'll try not to be too long. If I can find a farm house with a phone then I won't have to drive all the way back to Volterra. The hovel up in the field doesn't look like there would be a phone." He looked at his watch. "It's after three now. Hopefully, I should be back within the hour."

He bent down and searched through Phil's pockets to get the car keys. With the movement, blood started to flow more freely through the makeshift bandage. a red pool formed on the plastic sheet. Doug took off his belt and tightened it around Philip's thigh. He lifted off the bandage to check on the bleeding and dried the pool with his handkerchief. Margaret had another square of shirt cotton ready to replace the bloody one. "How often should I check this while you're gone?"

"Just loosen the belt about every ten minutes." Doug advised. "I think I'll light a fire so we can find you again in all this brush." He climbed back up the hill to replenish the pile of stakes while she found a cigarette lighter in Philip's sack to coax a flame on the tissue and an old envelope from her shoulder bag.

Margaret stood and hugged him. "Goodbye dear. Be careful." She watched him set off across the barren hillside on a downward course that would take him to the parked car. He disappeared from her sight and she gazed around at the terrain in awe of the tremendous forces of nature that had stripped away an entire forest. No birds sang now. A deathly stillness reigned all around her and she turned her attention to the man lying at her feet. His skin colour had changed to ashen and she wondered about the possibility of internal bleeding. "Oh God! Don't let him die here in front of me … Please! Don't let him die at all!"

She knelt down beside him and reached to feel his cold hands. Knowing the few remaining stakes would not last long in a fire, she climbed the hill back to the excavation and returned with another armload of dry wood. She attempted to break the stakes on a rock, and after some effort, she soon had a bonfire blazing nearby.

She moved closer to the warmth and checking on the tourniquet she was relieved to see the bleeding had not increased and checking her watch, she, realized the hour for Doug's absence had now become two and it was almost five o'clock! Wondering what was keeping him, she climbed back up the hill to get another load of wood. By the time she returned, cool shadows were growing all around and she shivered in fear as much as in the dropping temperature. She found physical comfort in the fire and emotional comfort as well because she knew it served as a beacon. "I'm glad I don't believe in ghosts" she mused looking at her surroundings.

Philip lay quietly, the extra sweater tucked around his head. She felt his hands again and thought they felt warmer than before. "Oh God, please send Doug back soon. It's going to be dark and I don't want to be here alone. I know You're here, and Phil's here too but he needs help and I don't want him to die …"

Darkness crept across the hillside and she huddled by the fire praying that help would soon come. The only sounds to be heard were the crackling of the sticks in the fire and an occasional sigh from Phil. Then she heard footsteps and voices from above and her heart flooded with relief. "Doug?"

Soon, a rough, bearded man and a young boy and a black shaggy dog came into view. They slid down to the campsite and viewed her situation. She attempted to explain but quickly realized they did not understand a word she was saying. They conversed between themselves after she showed them Philip's leg in its splint and before long, the boy squatted beside the fire with the dog while the man climbed back up the hill.

She judged the lad to be about six or seven. His large dark eyes under a shock of black hair regarded her suspiciously. She pointed to herself and said, "Margaret."

He seemed to understand because he pointed to himself and said, "Paulo."

When she smiled, he asked, "English?"

She replied, "Canadian."

He nodded and that seemed to be the last of the conversation. After a few minutes, she pointed to Philip and said his name. Paulo asked, "Canadian?"

"No, English."

That seemed to give the lad reason for contemplation so he sat for some time staring into the flames. Margaret looked at her watch again and saw it was now almost seven o'clock. "Oh, Doug … Where are you?"

The silent vigil seemed interminable as Margaret knelt by Philip watching him breathe. His cheeks were warm in spite of the cool air and she grew assured that he was not about to die after all. An hour had passed and then she heard the sounds of more people descending sideways on the slope. Another wave of relief flooded her being and several men bearing large flashlights and knapsacks and a litter arrived at the fireside. She frowned realizing that Doug was not with them. Two were obviously medical aides who quickly turned their attention to Philip while another, who wore a dark green uniform and cap, approached Margaret. "I am Cassini. I am with the local police. And so, Signora, your husband has been badly hurt in the landslide?"

She shook her head. "This man is not my husband. My husband left us four hours ago to find help. He went to get the car at the bottom of the hill in the parking area. Haven't you heard from him?"

"No Madame. Signor Montcelli, the farmer. Informed us of your plight." His eyes narrowed suspiciously. "We have not seen or heard from a husband."

Margaret drew a deep breath. "We didn't think the parking lot was very far away. Could my husband have got lost in the woods?" She could not imagine that likelihood but at this point, she realized anything was possible.

"Perhaps." He spoke slowly and Margaret wondered if he doubted her story. She turned as one of the aides came to speak to Cassini. Their conversation lasted only a minute before Cassini took out his cell phone and began speaking rapidly. He turned to her. "And your husband's name, Signora?"

"Parker, Douglas Parker."

"And your car?" She shook her head and pointed toward the stretcher. "The car belongs to him, to Philip Longfellow." She fumbled in the bag for his wallet and managed to find some documents that looked like vehicle registrations and licences. Cassini examined them under his flashlight and spoke rapidly into the phone again. He put the phone back into his pocket and said, "The medics are going to carry your friend down the hill. The ambulance will move around to the parking area. We will see if the car is still there and then we will know if your husband is still in the area."

Margaret's head began to throb. 'Does he think that my husband has abandoned us? What does he think has been happening here?' She watched as Paulo's father helped the medics move Philip onto the stretcher who cried out in pain. *He must be regaining consciousness. Thank God for that.*

Cassini remained by the fire watching them and Margaret out of the corner of his eye. "I think, Signora, we will accompany them down the hill now. We will extinguish this fire and be on our way." His cell phone rang and he answered it, his eyes narrowing again. The litter bearers were moving away across the denuded hillside with Paulo in front lighting the way. Cassini hung up his phone. "The car is still in the parking lot," he said bluntly.

"Then Doug's still here somewhere," she said. "What could have happened to him? Where did he go?"

"We will find him Signora. Let us go now."

"But I should stay here by the fire? He'll see the fire …"

The barking dog interrupted her protests. She heard shouting but could not understand what the man was saying. Cassini turned and hurried off across the slope. An anxious Margaret remained by the fire, wondering what was happening and praying that nothing had happened to Doug. Paulo came running up the hill and took her hand, tugging frantically. "Venite. Venite, Signora."

They had only gone a short distance over a rise when she saw in the torchlight the group of men standing around the stretcher lying once again on the ground. Wondering as she drew nearer, she then saw Cassini stretched flat on his stomach with his head down a hole. The dog pranced beside him wagging its tail.

"What is it?" she asked.

Cassini turned to look up at her. "I think we have found your husband. Lie down here and look. Be very careful though. You must distribute your weight."

He rose slowly and handed her the flashlight. Her mind was numb as she lay down and shone the light into a deep cavity in the earth. Doug lay slumped against a rock, his head fallen to one side, his eyes closed.

She fought the impulse to scream as a strange quietness closed round her and she felt as in a dream. Calling his name softly as though she was rousing him from a long nap, she watched his limp body. He did not respond.

Cassini broke into her nightmare. "This is your husband?"

A dreadful wave of fear washed over her and she groaned, "Yes …"

"Well, Signora. He looks to be in a bad way … We will have to get him out of here, but how …"

He began talking on his cell phone again as Margaret remained lying on the ground and staring at Doug. She moved the flashlight beam around the dusty cavity and discovered brightly coloured wall paintings, an array of furniture, pottery and two sarcophagi. *A tomb! Oh God! Doug's in a tomb!* She quickly shone the light back to his chest to see if he was breathing." Please God … He can't be dead … No. Not now."..

She began to weep and the streaming tears dropped into the chamber below. She turned to sit up. "Please, Mr. Cassini. I want to go down there to be with him," she sobbed.

"It is not possible now, Signora. We must wait for more help to arrive." He turned to direct the medics to carry the stretcher down to the waiting ambulance. Paulo came to stand by Margaret and put his arm around her waist while the dog tried to nose his way between them. "Oh Paulo," she cried, "I don't know what to do …"

The boy's dark eyes commiserated his understanding of her predicament and he patted her arm.. Cassini returned to the scene and stood apart from them. "I think Signora that we must be very careful here. The landslide has scraped away much of the layer of earth over this tomb. We do not want more of the ceiling to give way …" He spoke briefly to Paulo and the boy moved to his side with the dog.

She wiped her eyes with her sleeve. "Do you think my husband is… is dead?" A hiccup punctuated her question.

"It is hard to say. How long since he left you and Signor Longfellow?"

She shone the flashlight on her wrist watch and tried to remember. "Over four hours … Yes. He left after three o'clock and now it's almost eight." She began to weep again. "He's been lying here all this time …"

"And you didn't hear him call or cry out …"

She shook her head.

Paulo's father was breathing heavily as he climbed back up the hill to join them. Cassini and he conversed for a few moments and when Cassini took out his cell phone again, Margaret lay back down to watch her husband's body once more. Small clods of earth gave way around the edge of the hole and plummeted to the floor deep below and her bleary eyes peering through the glittering dust particles were unable to detect any movement of his chest. "Oh God," she murmured repeatedly, willing Doug to live. Her neck grew sore but she remained prone above the tomb with a sense of desperation to guard his life with her prayers.

Another plump man joined them shortly, his strength drained completely by the exertion of climbing the steep path. Margaret turned her head to watch him speaking to Cassini. The policeman called gently to her. "Please Signora. This is Signor Riccato, the curator of the museum. Would you allow him to look at the tomb?"

She studied the man's girth and replied, "Is there a possibility that he might collapse more of the ceiling?"

Cassini spoke to the curator who seemed affronted by the conversation and then replied, "He is not afraid of that, Signora."

"Perhaps he isn't, but I am. I don't want anything else falling on Doug." The curator was rubbing his hands and she wondered if he was cold or it was the anticipation of seeing the tomb. Reluctantly, she sat up and shifted herself away from the hole. Signor Riccato managed to ungracefully crawl toward the opening and his first reaction of wonderment evolved quickly to ecstasy.

Cassini translated his joyful utterances for Margaret. "He says this is a priceless find. There are so many urns, so many chests and all intact … He says it is a royal tomb … There will be much treasure here …" Cassini seemed to realize the significance of the find and started dialing numbers again and giving orders to the person on the other end of the line.

Margaret was looking at her watch again when several more men arrived carrying an odd assortment of pipes and ropes as well as large lanterns. Signor Riccato reluctantly left his viewing post as these men went to work erecting two tripods some distance from either side of the hole. More men arrived and judging from their animated conversation with Signor Riccato, Margaret guessed they too dealt in antiquities. Then three more men arrived with a stretcher and cases of medical equipment. A television cameraman and reporter appeared and the once desolate hillside now seemed very crowded.

Remembering she had left the knapsack by the fire, Margaret turned off her flashlight and slipped into the darkness. The embers still glowed so she was able to make her way up the slope and retrieve Phil's belongings. The air seemed cooler and fresher here on the heights and she rubbed her face to wipe away the grimy tearstains. "Oh God … Thank You for bringing all these people to help. Please let Doug still be alive … Just let me hold him again..".

She scuffed the embers with a piece of wood to cover them with dirt, and turning on her flashlight, made her way down the slope again. Assaulted by the reporter and the cameraman, Margaret endeavoured to tell them what had happened but she was distracted continually by the efforts to rescue Doug. She remembered seeing the same sort of contrivance on a smaller scale in McGuire's garage as the mechanics lifted an engine out of a truck. Now these men had erected a larger model because of the need for a greater expanse of room. Afraid of collapsing the ceiling they spread themselves out as they adjusted a pulley on the cross pipe. Then the smallest member of the group put one foot into a sling and they lowered him into the cavity. Margaret held her breath while they strained at the rope and when they stood up she knew the fellow had reached the floor. A shout ascended and Cassini took her elbow. "He says he's still alive," he murmured.

Her knees buckled and Cassini's grasp tightened. "We will get him out now," he said. A small medic was also lowered into the hole and was soon followed by the basket type of stretcher that Margaret had seen used for injured skiers on television. She bit her lip and chewed the tip of her finger as the minutes passed in a deathly silence. "What is taking them so long … What are they doing to him?" she whispered to Cassini.

Cassini summoned another medic and directed him to inquire at the hole. He returned shortly to report. Cassini turned to Margaret. "Your husband has a dislocated shoulder among other injuries and they have just reset it so they could get him into the stretcher. He will be coming up shortly."

She drew a deep breath. "Other injuries? Did he say what else was wrong?"

"A broken collar bone … The unconsciousness means a concussion or some other type of head injury. Perhaps there is other internal damage..?"

More men carrying large cases arrived at the scene accompanied by uniformed officers. Cassini said, "Now we have a guard for this place. It will be very busy here for a long time. Ah … Here comes your husband now."

The men heaved on the rope in unison and gradually pulled the stretcher to the surface. Doug was bound tightly in place and as he emerged from the ground a cheer went up from the crowd. The medic caught the bottom of the stretcher and pulled it away from the hole and the ropes released it to settle on the ground. Margaret rushed to his side and gazed at his pale face. "Oh my darling …"

The medic spoke to Cassini who interpreted. "We are going to take him to the hospital in Siena. Volterra is closer but Siena has better facilities for this type of injury."

"I will go with him in the ambulance," Margaret stated.

After a brief conversation Cassini said, "That will not be possible, Signora. There is no room for you. They want to do some medical tests on your husband and you will have to follow behind."

Margaret frowned, "Where did they take Signor Longfellow?"

Cassini replied, "They took him to Volterra but he, too, has been transferred to Siena."

"Could you find someone to drive me to the hospital in Signor Longfellow's car? I'm too upset to concentrate on driving tonight on these roads."

Cassini smiled. "Of course. Do you have the keys?"

Margaret knelt beside the stretcher and fumbled beneath the blanket in Doug's pockets until she found them." Be well, my darling. Be well. God is here too and He will take care of you." She kissed his forehead and stood up as the medics came alongside again.

Led by a fellow bearing a large torch, four men carried the stretcher down into the darkness. Thanking Cassini, Margaret hurried after them accompanied by a young police officer. Treacherously steep at times, the convoluted path eventually led them to the crowded parking lot where the ambulance waited with a flashing red light. The events of the day had exhausted Margaret to the point where she had to wrack her brain to remember what Philip's car looked like, and in the darkness, all those cars seemed the same. After several attempts, she found a door lock that the key in her hand fit into and checking the contents of the trunk, she gave the keys to the young man and said, "This is it."

He smiled and motioned her to the passenger seat. The ambulance was already backing out of the parking lot and Margaret sighed as their car took off in pursuit. "Do you speak English?" she asked.

His raised eyebrows and hand gesture indicated that he was not familiar with the language and she decided not to distract him with conversation. The steep, winding inclines that were hair-raising by day were only worse at night and by the time they reached the outskirts of Siena, Margaret knew first-hand the meaning of white knuckle driving. Her foot and ankle were sore from braking constantly on the steep turns of the road. The narrow streets of Siena wound up hills too, and when they pulled into the parking lot of the hospital, the driver had to apply the parking brake because of the slope. He brought Margaret inside, gave her the keys and nodded goodbye.

She thought she had stepped back in time as she looked around at the stark waiting room with high ceilings, tall opaque glass windows, wooden chairs, a single suspended white glass globe that shone on the white painted walls. She walked over to stand beside a vacant reception desk and wondered how long it would take for someone to come and deal with her. Scuffed swinging doors at the end of a short hallway intimidated her but after some time she decided to take the risk and pushed one open to look down a long hall. She recognized a medic and walked toward him. "What's happening? Where's Mr. Parker?"

He spoke to someone inside the treatment room and a gray, wrinkled nurse emerged. Margaret judged her to be at least fifty and wondered about her skills. "Do you speak English?" she asked.

"Yes. You are Mrs. Parker?"

The nurse's quiet voice calmed Margaret's rapidly beating heart.

"Yes. What is happening … Where is he?"

"The doctor is with him now. He is ordering several x-rays. Your husband seems to be in stable condition. We will know more about his injuries in a few hours."

"May I see him now?"

The nurse led Margaret into the room where Doug lay on a stretcher. The doctor straightened up from examining his patient's eyes. "I think your husband will recover, Signora. He is going to the radiology department now and if you will wait in his room, I will see you when I know the results."

As the medic wheeled the stretcher past Margaret she gazed at Doug's still form and wondered how long it would be before he opened his eyes. The nurse handed Margaret a brown paper bag containing his clothing and asked her to sign for the contents of the pockets and his watch and wedding ring. "We will go to his room now if you wish."

Taking an elevator to the third floor, she led Margaret along a quiet darkened corridor, passing an empty nursing station and semi-darkened patient rooms. "Here is 310" she said. "You can wait here for your husband. May I get you a cup of tea?"

"Thank you," Margaret said. "I would appreciate that very much. No milk or sugar, please."

The nurse left her standing in another white high ceilinged room with tall opaque glass windows, two white metal beds with white coarse linen spreads, two white metal washstands.. She gave Margaret a face cloth and a hand towel and a bar of soap, and indicated a small sink in the corner. "You will want to freshen up."

Margaret looked at her tired face with muddy tear stained cheeks in the mirror over the small sink where she washed her grubby hands. She pushed an old brown vinyl recliner closer to the bed to sink into this chair and close her eyes. The light from the two florescent fixtures at the head of the beds still glared into her eyes and she rose to pull the string on the one in front of her. *What a day! Oh Doug ... You've got to get better so we can get out of here. I just want to go home to New Lancaster ... I don't like mountains anymore, mountains and hills. I'm becoming paranoid I guess ... I don't like little airplanes, cramped spaces ...* She heard the nurse returning and opened her eyes.

"Here you are, Mrs. Parker." She placed a tray on one of the bedside tables. "The charge nurse will be along shortly to get some information from you."

"Thank you."

"There has been a reporter asking for you, too. Would you care to talk to him now?"

Margaret sighed and stood up. "Would it seem selfish for me to say no? I am very tired and I would really like to wait to see how my husband is before I say anything. Could he come back in the morning?"

The wrinkled face smiled. "Of course. I understand you have had quite an ordeal. I will explain this to him. Good night, Mrs. Parker."

Margaret slipped out of her shoes and poured herself a cup of tea. Munching on a biscuit she thought of Philip Longfellow and wondered if he had regained consciousness and notified his friend here in Siena. She turned her head at the sound of approaching footsteps and a square-set nurse entered the room. The woman wore a starched white uniform, and a stiff cap perched atop her black curls

"Good evening, Mrs. Parker. I am Sister Pagano and I need to get some information from you about your husband." She flipped open a chart and began to take the particulars about the health and life of Douglas Parker. Margaret produced their health insurance cards and said she would have to telephone the company in the morning after she had talked with the doctor.

As nurse Pagano was leaving the room, Margaret asked, "Would you know if Philip Longfellow has been admitted here this afternoon?"

"Yes," she replied. "He's in Room 312. He's just come up from surgery a short time ago."

"Thank you," Margaret said as the nurse bustled out into the hall.

Sipping her tea, she decided to peek into Phil's room and see if he was sleeping yet. Approaching the door she could hear a low voice and as she moved into the darkened room she heard a male voice saying, "Philip, dear heart. What would I do without you? I've never loved anyone like I love you."

Philip sighed in response.

The smooth male voice said, "*Good night sweet prince. May flights of angels sing thee to thy rest*." Shocked beyond measure!.... *Oh God! What else? Philip has a lover! I wonder if Doug knows about this. They did spend some time together ... I won't say anything to him about it now. Later will be soon enough.*

She fell asleep sitting in the chair with the empty mug on her lap and, when wakened much later by the stretcher bumping into the bed, she jumped up and for a moment wondered where she was. Doctor Matera introduced himself to Margaret as the orderlies and nurse transferred Doug to the bed. An intravenous bottle hung on a pole beside the bed and a catheter drainage bottle dangled on another hook below. The doctor rubbed his chin sprouting a new day's stubble. "Mr. Parker has a cracked collar bone and we have put him in a temporary brace. His shoulder was dislocated and there is a large bruise. He will need some therapy for that in a few days. I am giving him antibiotics to prevent a possible pneumonia resulting from his long exposure to the cold floor in the tomb. The x-rays have showed no further injury. The CAT scan of the brain showed no haematoma or swelling. Now, do you have any questions?"

"Why is he still unconscious?"

"There is obviously a small concussion but Mr. Parker should regain consciousness soon. I will be back in the morning to check on him."

Margaret watched as the nurse checked Doug one more time and raised one of the sides of the bed. "Will you be staying here for a while, Mrs. Parker?"

Realizing she had no where else to go, Margaret said. "Yes, I'll be here."

The nurse nodded and turned to leave. "Use the call button if there's any change."

Margaret drew a chair up to the bedside and sat down, taking Doug's hand in one of hers and stroking his forearm with the other. "Oh Doug," she whispered. "Please wake up soon and tell me you are going to be well again." She lay her head down on the bed and praying, fell asleep.

Wakened by the sounds of trolleys in the hall she raised her head to see faint sunshine through the window. Doug remained comatose and she rose to kiss his cheek and stroke his brow with a sense of dread for his condition. Another nurse arrived to check his vital signs and directed Margaret to a washroom down the corridor. The ward was stirring with more activity and Margaret returned to sit in the lounge chair and contemplate their situation. *I should call someone but who? Michael? Ann? Oh God … in a foreign country It's so awful to be alone… But I'm not alone …You're here. Help me to think clearly, God. I'm so tired.* She lay her head back and closed her eyes. *I'll have to call the insurance company … And I should find out about Philip. Perhaps he would know what to do … Oh God, I don't want to go in that room and find him with his lover … But what else can I do, God?"*

She dozed for a short time before being interrupted by a nurse bringing her a tray. "I've brought you some breakfast, Signora. There is a reporter from Paris who wants to speak with you"

At the sight of a large bowl of oatmeal and a boiled egg, Margaret thanked Sister Pagano and said "Would you please tell him, I'll be free after breakfast.". Hungry, she ate the oatmeal and found it very nourishing She nibbled at the roll, and the hot strong coffee revived her energy. When Dr. Matera arrived on his rounds of the ward, he expressed his concern that Doug had not regained consciousness. "I don't understand this, Mrs. Parker," he said after testing Doug's reflexes and examining his eyes. "There is no reason on earth why your husband should not be awake." He shook Doug's uninjured shoulder and said loudly into his ear, "Wake up, Mr. Parker! Wake up!"

There was no response. Margaret bit her fingertip and held her breath as Dr. Matera pinched Doug's cheeks and then lightly slapped them. He turned to her. "I will return later. I want to consult my colleagues."

Alone again, Margaret drew close to the bedside and whispered, "Wake up, darling." She began to weep and lay her head down near the pillow. "Oh Jesus … Please help Doug. Save him from whatever is wrong … Please Jesus, I don't know what else to say … Just save him from whatever is keeping him in this state …"

Doug drew a deep breath and uttered a long moan as he exhaled. Margaret drew back in amazement and then bent down again. "Wake up, darling. Wake him up, Jesus,. Keep him going …"

Doug sighed again and she continued to urge him back to reality by stroking his cheeks and rubbing his hands. "You're going to be all right, darling. You're going to be all right. Jesus is here with us and He's helping you."

A tear rolled down Doug's cheek and she wiped it with the sheet. "Come on, darling. Wake up now …"

His chest began to heave and she thought it sounded as though he was crying inside. She continued to stroke his face and arm. "That's it, darling. Jesus is here. He's helping you … You're going to be fine."

Doug began to move his legs and when he attempted to sit up, he cried out with the pain in his shoulder. His eyes opened wide and before some of the nursing staff had run into the room, he had collapsed and cried, "Oh God!"

"I'm here, Doug, I'm here," Margaret continued to murmur into his ear as tears coursed down his cheeks.

Nurse Pagano on the other side of the bed watched and dispatched another nurse to find Dr. Matera. "We can't give you anything for the pain, Mr. Parker, until the doctor comes.

His crying subsided and he turned to Margaret. "Don't leave me," he croaked. "Please don't leave me."

"Shh darling. Of course I won't leave you … I'll stay right here."

A nurse brought a basin of warm water and bathed his face. Another nurse cranked up the head of the bed and Doug was able to look around now. "Where are we?" he asked Margaret.

"A hospital in Siena."

"And Phil?"

"He's across the hall … He's going to be okay too …"

Dr. Matera strode into the room. "So you've decided to join us, Mr. Parker …"

Doug looked at Margaret. "You were unconscious for a long time, dear," she explained. "Dr. Matera couldn't find any reason for your being in a coma."

"Yes," Dr. Matera added. "You've escaped having a very serious injury considering the height you'd fallen."

Doug narrowed his eyes.

"You've become a famous man, falling into an Etruscan tomb. From all reports, the find is quite spectacular and archaeologists are descending on Volterra in droves."

As Dr. Matera explained Doug's injuries to him and his prognosis, Margaret watched her husband closely, detecting a tense vulnerability she had never seen before. His twitching fingers often plucked at the blanket and she noticed a tic in his cheek and he was blinking his eyes rapidly as well. "… And I think another day or two in the hospital before you are discharged. Now, nurse, we'll remove all these tubes and get Mr. Parker something to eat."

Margaret went down to the business office to straighten out Doug's account and on her return tapped on the partially closed door of 312. Philip Longfellow raised his head to greet her and she inquired after his health. "I have a broken leg and some cracked ribs. They were doing some blood tests to see if I had a ruptured spleen and liver but that seems to be settling down now so I should be on the mend soon." Margaret noticed his leg wrapped in a tensor bandage with wires protruding and lying in a cradle sling with ropes and pulleys dangling at the end of his bed

Philip wiped his perspiring brow and said," I hear Doug made quite a find yesterday. How's he doing?"

"He has a very sore shoulder and a cracked collar bone. The doctor says he can go home in a day or so. If he feels like it later we may come over here to visit you."

Philip nodded and Margaret crossed the hall to find Doug was reclining in front of a breakfast tray. "You're not eating, dear?" she asked.

"I've lost my appetite. Come here and let me hold you. I need to feel you close to me."

She moved alongside the bed and put one arm across his chest and lay her head on the hollow of his neck.

"I must have got an awful whack on the head," he said at last. "I've never felt like this in my life ... the dreams, the fantasies. It was horrible ..."

She patted his chest. "I imagine it was. I can scarcely believe what we've been through in the last twenty-four hours ... And to think you were so near to me and I didn't know it. I was worried about Phil and never dreamed you were in trouble too ... I'm going to have to move, Doug. I'm getting a crick in my neck." She stood up and moved the chair to the bedside so she could still hold his arm.

He cleared his throat. "I think I've lived a lifetime in the last twenty-four hours. I want to tell you all this now because I know I'll forget it ... Even now some of it is hazy ..."

She leaned toward him, her face solemn. "Then tell me ..."

"I remember hurrying across the hillside and feeling the ground crumbling beneath my feet, and falling down, down, down through space for an interminable length of time … I was thinking that I should soon reach the bottom of wherever l was but I kept falling … And the darkness … It seemed so intense … I could hardly breathe … I had that awful sensation of falling, of emptiness, and then I realized there was nothing to feel anymore. I had lost contact with everything and I was completely alone. It was horrible …"

He shut his eyes tightly and squeezed her fingers. "I don't want to remember …"

"Then don't, darling. It was just a bad dream."

"I don't even think it was a nightmare. It was so real. Is it possible I was in another dimension?"

Margaret shook her head. "I don't know anything about that kind of stuff."

"Could I have been in hell?"

She frowned. "I don't think so, dear."

"Hell couldn't be any worse than where I was. If there was fire then there would have been light … And anything would have been better than the darkness …"

"Oh Doug …"

He opened his eyes. "And now I remember something else … I wasn't alone. Oh God! There was this presence! … And I felt it was sticking to me. I tried to pull away but it wouldn't let me go! It was like glue and I was filled with terror. I tried to see what it was but I couldn't open my eyes! And it was sucking me down, down into the darkness. Oh hold me, Margaret. Don't let it get me!"

Unable to fathom his terror, Margaret held his head close to hers and tried to calm him. "Shh, darling. Nothing is going to get you. You're here with me now. You're safe and sound. Jesus is here and He won't let anything happen to you."

Doug began to cry and she continued to stroke his head and kiss his cheek. "It's alright, darling. It's alright."

When he stopped heaving, she wiped his cheeks with the sheet and smiled into his eyes. "You've had a very bad time, haven't you …

But it's over now and we're going to get out of here and go home and never think about all this.. again."

His voice seemed strangled as he said, "I'll never forget this because do you know what brought me back to you?"

She frowned.

"I heard you saying the name of Jesus … And when I heard that, it seemed as though that awful presence started to lose its grip on me. I felt it leaving and I stopped falling and then the darkness seemed to recede and I was here with you. I think I was in hell, Margaret … or very close to it. The name of Jesus saved me … He brought me back again."

Margaret continued to stare at him. "Do you really think so?"

"Yes."

"Look … Let's just take some time to get you better, and in a few days, you can see if you still feel the same way. Let's just be content for now with the fact that Jesus is here taking care of us."

Doug picked at the sheet. "I remember you told me about asking Jesus to save you …You know, repenting of your sins and trusting him as your Saviour. I thought I had done all that, but perhaps I hadn't, not really. Now I know Jesus has saved me from hell but I want to make sure He knows I know it, So Jesus, if you're still listening to me, and I know You are, I want to confess to You right now that I am a sinner and I'm asking You to be my Saviour. Will You come and live in my heart and show me what You want me to do with the rest of my life? And I'll thank You forever for saving me from hell."

Fresh tears were running down his cheeks and Margaret began to weep too as she heard her husband really pray for the first time. *Thank You, God. Thank You, Jesus. Thank You, Spirit for bringing Doug to Yourself. Out of all this terrible situation You have brought Good and thank You again for what You are doing in our lives.*

They continued to cling to each other for a long time as the Presence of the Lord bound them together in the wonder of His mighty power. Finally, Margaret drew away. "I'm getting a crick in my neck again. You're going to have to get out of that bed or I'm coming in there with you."

Doug smiled. "There isn't any room for you so I'll get up instead."

"We'd better get the nurse to help. Your shoulder must be pretty sore."

"Actually, it isn't too bad. I feel a little woozy so they must be giving me some pain-killers."

The nurse produced an old wooden wheel chair and as they went out to the hallway a young man, clad in denim with a camera dangling around his neck introduced himself as Gordon Jenson from the Rome office of the Associated Press. He also mentioned he would be putting their story on the wire and it would no doubt be picked up by Time Magazine and asked permission to take Doug's picture After a very short interview, they parted as Margaret pushed the ancient contraption across the hall to see Philip and was greatly relieved to find him alone. He opened his eyes as they approached. "So Douglas, I hear you have made the archaeological find of the century."

A gentleman arrived at the door of the room.. Margaret was sure he was Philip's lover. Dressed in a grey silk woolen suit the man was impeccably groomed, and as Philip introduced Fredrico Scalise, the Parkers were impressed by his demeanour. His silver hair, combed back off his tanned forehead and his freshly shaved cheeks and chin bespoke some professional care. He thanked them graciously for their care of his dear friend and assured them of his aid in any way. Margaret mentioned their health insurance company would need some information and Fredrico assured them he would take care of it at once, and Doug said he would like to contact his children in Canada and Kenya. Fredrico inquired "Would you use the telephone or the E mail?"

Doug cleared his throat and said, "I don't feel up to talking to anyone now so I'll just dictate a message to the family. Margaret? Will you get some paper from the nurse and we can work on it when we go back to my room?"

Fredrico smiled. "I'm sure there must be something I can help you with. Where are you staying?"

Margaret replied "Yes, thank you very much. I must contact the office of our insurance company and let them know what has happened. Oh, by the way our hotel is the Lido in Tarquinia."

Fredrico glanced at Philip and said, "My dear Mrs. Parker, just give me your card or papers and I will take care of it for you this morning. and I presume you have not been back to your hotel since the accident." He paused and turned to Doug and said

"Because of all the notoriety, you may be besieged at your hotel. I suggest it might be better if you were to move into the condominium that Philip and I share. It is just down the promenade from your hotel."

Philip turned his head to Doug and said," That's a wonderful idea. Doug. We can offer you some privacy."

Margaret opened her purse. "I must give you the keys to your car, Philip. :It's in the parking lot on the hill, just outside the hospital.;"."

Fredrico held out his hand. "I'll take care of the car, Mrs. Parker now. If you would like, I'll drive you over to my home and you can write your messages to the family. Do you have their e-mail addresses?"

She turned to Doug. "Do we?"

He shook his head. "You have their telephone numbers in your book. Just call them and ask if they can give you an address.. Be sure to tell Anne and Michael I'll talk to them in a few days, when I feel up to it."

Fredrico said, "Shall we go, Mrs Parker?"

She turned to him and smiled, "Please, Call me Margaret."

He took her elbow and guided her into the corridor as Philip and Doug began rehearsing the events of the previous day. They took the elevator to the ground floor and Fredrico said, "Dr Matera wants to see me about Philip, so can you wait for me at the emergency entrance?"

"Of course.".

The reception area seemed very crowded in contrast to the empty room where Margaret had arrived the night before. A large tour bus was parked in the street outside the doors of the hospital. She noticed a red maple leaf on a white background of a flag pasted on a rear window. "Canadians!" she murmured and left Fredrico, to walk outside and look at the bus. The bus driver stood at the door to the bus smoking a cigarette "Are you really from Canada?" she asked

"No, Firenza." he replied. These tourists say they are from the R O M."

"R O M?" she asked "Is that in Canada?" I never heard of it."

The bus driver stared at her. "I think they mean Toronto."

The RO M in Toronto! The meaning of it washed over her and she felt like an idiot. "Of course, the Royal Ontario Museum. This is a tour group from Toronto." She looked about wondering if there was a faint possibility that she might know someone. "So what has happened? Why are you at the hospital?"

"This morning, the tour director's wife fell outside the hotel and she broke her wrists on the curb. I must find the director because we are late to our next destination. Here he comes now."

Much to Margaret's total amazement, her former pastor emerged from the hospital and walked toward her.. "Margaret Darwin! of all people! What are you doing here in Siena? You seem to appear at the strangest of times," he said, remembering their chance meeting at the station with Peter Spencer, on the train heading north to New Lancaster almost a year ago..

She grasped his hand. "What are you doing in Italy, Mr. Pearson? The bus driver told me your wife injured her wrists in a fall. How is Bridget? We used to play bridge together."

Jim Pearson smiled, "Poor old Birdie was quite bored with our retirement at Chapel Lake, and I answered an advertisement for someone to lead a group of people on a tour of old cathedrals and churches in Europe. I couldn't resist the offer of a free trip but I didn't count on the rough sidewalks in Italy. It's a miracle that more of these old dears haven't hurt themselves. So, Margaret, what are you doing over here?"

She smiled deliciously at him. "I'm on my honeymoon. We stopped here on our way home from Kenya. My husband is a school teacher in New Lancaster. Your friend John Copse officiated at our wedding just before he died. Isn't it a small world!"

Jim patted her hand. "Margaret, I'm in a terrible rush. I'm sorry I have to leave you right now because the tour is late for meeting our guide at the Duomo of Siena. It's just at the top of the street. But I don't know what to do about Bridget. She's getting her fractures mended and Dr. Matera says with casts on she'll be able to travel too. I hate to leave her here, but I've got to get the group on the bus up to the Duomo."

Margaret patted his hand. "Don't you worry about Bridget, Jim. I'll go in to stay with her and bring her up to join the tour as soon as she is ready. I know Dr. Matera, because he's been treating my husband after his fall. Our friend will give Bridget a ride in his car to the Duomo. She doesn't want to climb any more hills and neither do I."

Jim looked at Margaret sympathetically. "So your husband had a tumble too. I think we should do all our travelling while we are still young enough to survive the rigours of adventure. Where did your husband have his trouble?"

She watched his eyes open in astonishment when she replied, "Oh, he dropped about twenty feet into an Etruscan tomb near Volterra."

They proceeded into the hospital and found Mrs. Pearson in a small treatment room lying on a gurney while Dr. Matera examined a series of X rays on a bank of screens along the wall. He pointed to the fractures showing Mr.. Pearson the damage. A nurse entered, bearing a tray with some medication for her patient and turned to bring out a basin of water and a box of plaster bandages. Margaret took advantage of the interval to learn Dr. Matera had still not had his interview with Fredrico and she said quietly to the Pearsons that she would return very shortly to accompany Bridget to join the tour.. When she left the room in search of Fredrico, she heard Jim Pearson attempting to comfort his wife "Poor Birdie, you've had such a hard time, my dear. I know all this walking and climbing has been too much for you. Our next holiday, we'll spend at Chapel Lake Lodge."

When Jim Pearson walked through the waiting room, Margaret slipped into the treatment room to watch as Dr. Matera skillfully wound the plaster bandages around Bridget's wrists. The nurse administered a hypodermic to Bridget who sighed as the procedure continued. While Dr. Matera washed his hands at the sink, Margaret came to his side and said, "Signor Scalise has an appointment with you this morning. Would you ask him to join me here while Mrs. Pearson rests before I take her to join her husband on the tour?

Dr. Matera dried his hands on a paper towel and smiled, "Of course. I'll send him in immediately You Canadian tourists are keeping me very busy."

Margaret turned to Bridget and patted her shoulder, "Do you feel well enough to walk?" As Bridget nodded, she asked the nurse, "Could you fix up a sling for Mrs. Pearson's arms?

After the nurse had adjusted the sling, Fredrico Scalise entered the room, rubbing his cheeks. "Are you ready to go, Margaret?"

"Yes…. May I introduce you to an old friend of mine from Toronto, She and her husband are on a tour of old churches and cathedrals in Europe. Bridget fell outside their hotel this morning and broke both of her wrists. Dr. Matera just patched her up. I told her husband that we would take her to join the tour of the Duomo of Siena. He said it was up at the top of the street. Would you mind?"

Fredrico smiled, "I'll get the car and bring it around to the door and you can wait there on the sidewalk for me." He touched the brim of his fedora and left them as Margaret took Bridget's arm to help her off the treatment table and they went out to the bright sunshine of late morning The car arrived as Bridget said, "Margaret, I can't believe this is happening….to think we are half way around the world and here we are meeting like this. What are you doing in Italy?"

'I'm on my honeymoon. My husband had a bad fall and he's upstairs in this hospital and we met Mr. Scalise because his friend was more or less involved in the same accident. I won't go into all the details but here's the car, so let's go see this wonderful cathedral."

The wonderful cathedral was an imposing edifice of polychrome marble. with ornate columns and arches and turrets. Fredrico drove past the intricate facade to park beside the bus standing in the shadow of a tall bell tower with a striking arrangement of black and white marble on the walls of the structure.. He stepped out of the car to consult with the bus driver who was smoking another cigarette.

Bridget turned to Margaret and whispered "Just look at that man! All he has wanted to do since he started driving our bus in Rome is smoke. Some of us sitting in the front seats asked him politely not to smoke."

Margaret laughed and said, "Perhaps you haven't noticed the roads and hills the poor man has to navigate. If I were in his place I'd probably be chain smoking too."

"I don't know what I'm going to do, Margaret. I feel completely helpless. Poor Jim is going to have to feed me, dress me and, when I go to the bathroom I won't be able to wipe my own bottom, and Jim can't come into the 'Ladies' with me."

Margaret nodded. "Is there a woman on the tour by herself? Perhaps she could help you?"

Bridget narrowed her eyes "As a matter of fact there is a woman, Helen? I think she used to be a nurse because she took charge of everything so carefully when I fell."

Margaret hugged Bridget "There's the answer to your problem. Let's find Jim and Helen, and explain what you're going to need." She waved to Fredrico and he walked toward them as they entered the cathedral through the central of three bronze portals and turned to see the tour group sitting in the carved wooden choir stalls gazing at the wide circular stained glass window of the Last Supper high above the front doors. The gothic arches lifted one's gaze heavenward past the black and white marble stripes on the walls. There were numerous plaster busts of sculpted animals on the marble columns which the tour guide was busy explaining the significance of the she-wolf, breast feeding Romulus and Remus, founders of Rome, who each had sired a son and the two cousins had founded Siena. Other columns of dark green marble and red marble were located at the front of the nave near an intricately carved pulpit. The tour guide was explaining that the group was fortunate to be present at Siena at this time because the mosaic tiled floor was only uncovered three weeks of the year. As the group descended from the choir loft to greet Bridget they gazed upon the inlaid marble mosaic floor, unique in Italy after two centuries of labour contributed by forty artists. Impressed by the beauty, the Canadians conferred in hushed tones as they were ushered into another chapel to view rare and priceless works of art from the thirteenth and fourteenth centuries. Jim came alongside and put his arm around his wife's waist "Do you feel well enough to continue Birdie?"

She nodded her head and said "Yes. These plaster casts are terribly heavy and I wish we could find the fiberglass kind. Dr Matera apologized because the hospital had run out of its supply, but Margaret's been a great help and I must speak to Helen for a minute."

Margaret looked about the cathedral and saw Fredrico examining the sculptures on the wall inside the portals. She said "Excuse me Bridget, but I really must go. I see my friend waiting for me." She shook Jim's hand and kissed Bridget's cheek in farewell. Hurrying to his side, she said, "I'm sorry to have kept you waiting. This is such a beautiful church. I'm glad to have had an opportunity to see it."

Fredrico took her arm and said, "You haven't seen the best part, my dear. We'll follow your friends now into the Piccolomini Library". The library at the Vatican had prepared Margaret for an unusual spectacle but she almost staggered at the stunning beauty of this library constructed to house the books and collection of manuscripts of Pope Pius III in the mid-fifteenth century. The tour group from the R O M listened to the guide with rapt expressions on their faces as they gazed upon the sculptures in the hall and in the arched niches with the richly coloured frescoes of biblical scenes on the walls. Margaret paused before a statue of a beautiful woman. Frederico said, "This is the patron saint of Siena, Catherine, who walked through the snowy mountain passes to Avignon in France to beg the Pope Urban to return to Rome where another pope, Clement Vll had claimed the papal throne fraudulently. This heroic act led to her beatification, among other miracles and heavenly visions, and after an early death, her body lies in the papal vaults in St. Peter's Basilica but her shrunken head is guarded carefully in the Basilica on the other side of this city."

Margaret gasped. "Her head! How? Why?"

Fredrico drew her outside to sit at a table at a sidewalk café overlooking the Piazza de Palio. "Italian history is confusing to most of us. At Catherine's time, the church in Rome was confronted by many challenges. Copernicus had brought forth his theory that the planet Earth was not the center of the universe. And for that he suffered. Then came Gallileo with his telescope to expound upon Copernicus' theory and to prove him right which turned the whole concept of the correct interpretation of scripture upside down. There were plagues, death and skirmishes among the seventy ducal states, so it became necessary to gain favour in the ecclesiastical. circles. At this same time, Urban, the Cardinal from Siena had been appointed the papal annunciata to the French court in Avignon. Meanwhile there was a power struggle back in Rome where another candidate for Pope, a Barberini, was elected, and his enemies immediately elected Urban in Avignon as the true and rightful pope. Because the Barberini family was disliked by most of the doges, Catherine rallied her followers to go to Avignon to persuade Urban to go to the Vatican to rid the papal seat of the one who was regarded as a barbarian. Tension was running very high and when Catherine died of a stroke at age thirty three, her followers wanted to take her body home to Siena but the new pope, Urban, wouldn't allow it, because he claimed she was to lie at his side when he himself died. Her supporters disobeyed his order and, unable to smuggle her body out of the city, they cut off her head and reverently brought it home to Siena in a bag where it now remains under the altar at the Basilica of San Domionico. Ercole Ferrata carved the statue for the Duomo two hundred years later."

Fredrico leaned back in his chair and rubbed his eyes" I've been talking too much and it's very warm in the sun. Would you care for something cold to drink?"

Margaret adjusted her sunglasses. "An iced tea would be nice."

Frederico signaled a waiter and mopped his brow with his handkerchief." When are you and Douglas planning to return to Canada?"

She smiled and said, "Not for ages, I hope. I'm having a wonderful time. Her cheeks reddened and guiltily she said, "I suppose we should wait until Doug feels well enough to travel."

Frederico drank his iced cappuccino and wiped his forehead. "I shouldn't drink this stuff so quickly. Now I've got a brain freeze. The reason I asked, is that you see a piazza before you here which is the site of the Palio, a horse race."

She raised her eye brows "Here? On this street with all these shops?"

Frederico smiled. "The shops close their doors and the crowd gathers in the center of the piazza. They only allow ten horses in the race. Siena is divided into seventeen wards. Each district has its own mascot,. a bear, or an eagle, a panther, or a dragon or some such way to identify itself with its racing colours and flags. They only race in July, and again in August. It's a vicious contest with the bare back jockeys flailing each other and if they fall off or, if their mount falls or crashes into a wall or post, the race continues at a peril to everyone else. There is a spectacular pageant that draws people from around the world to celebrate the religious festival of the Feast of the Assumption dedicated to the Virgin Mary.

"There is a marvelous parade the day before the first race with the police officers of Siena mounted on horseback wielding swords, the coloured banners of each ward flying above the crowd. It is a hotly contested race and the winner is the first horse to cross the finish line with its head ornament still intact."

The tour bus emitted clouds of smoke and ground gears on the incline and circled the piazza slowly and then disappeared down a side street as Margaret said "Doug will never believe that I met someone I knew from Toronto in this crowded country."

Fredrico fumbled in his jacket and found his silver framed sun glasses. "Is Toronto your home?"

"Not any longer," Margaret murmured. "I used to live there with my first husband and two sons. After my husband died, I moved to a small town in Northern Ontario and met Douglas who had lived there most of his life. We married several months ago and came to Italy on our honeymoon. We went to Kenya on the way to visit his son and family. His son is an agronomist with the U N. His daughter is a doctor in Toronto. I must call them on the telephone soon and let them know about their father before they read about it in the newspaper. A reporter from the Paris office of the Associated Press interviewed us in the hospital. He said he would put the story on the wire, whatever that means."

Fredrico smiled, "It means that very shortly everyone in the world will hear about Douglas falling into ancient history. And that means we had better get to my home and make your telephone calls."

Margaret hesitated. "I'm sure calls to Canada are expensive so I insist on paying you."

Fredrico tipped his hat back on his head and stood up. "I assure you, Signora, that will not be necessary. I am, how do you say, on an expense account?"

Chapter Three

FREDRICO OPENED THE passenger door of Philip's Fiat and Margaret slid onto the front seat. Having occupied the rear seat of the vehicle on the way from Tarquinia and driving to Siena in the dark, she had not realized the car was so small. The air conditioner blew cool air and made the interior much more comfortable. Fredrico wriggled his legs under the steering wheel and said, "Philips needs to get another car, his legs are much longer than mine." He backed cautiously out of the parking space beside the campanile into the tourist crowded market place and circled the piazza and turned on to the same side street the bus had taken. The narrow street was lined with shops and Margaret asked, "How did the bus ever squeeze along here?" She smiled at the lines of laundry strung overhead with a variety of suits of long underwear flapping in the breeze from the traffic.

Fredrico said, "At least the laundry remains intact. Occasionally a higher vehicle snags a line and you might see a furious woman chasing it to retrieve her clothing from the aerial or the roof of the truck. Many tenants seek to avoid the problem by renting the top floors. Have you been to Naples? It's quite a sight to see on laundry day. Some of the apartment buildings are ten stories or more."

"No," Margaret replied. "We haven't seen Naples yet, but I expect we will when we go to Pompeii. Doug wants to take the ferry to Capri."

Fredrico smiled. "You and your husband have many delights ahead. Italy is a wonderful country for seeing the sights. Are you planning to go into the north?".

She hesitated. "We haven't really decided yet. I think we should wait until Doug feels comfortable with driving in the infamous Italian traffic… Now with his shoulder injury, I don't know. Perhaps we can take a train or a bus. I would dearly love to see Florence and Venice and La Scala in Milan. I'm not sure Doug shares my passion for opera, but he does like to sing so I'm sure he'll go along with me on that plan."

Fredrico drove confidently, cruising in and out of lanes of slow moving trucks, laden with farm machinery, ploughs and carts. He turned the Fiat to the entrance to the auto strada pointing to Pisa and Milan.. "Oh," Margaret said "I thought you lived in Siena."

"Technically, I do," Fredrico smiled. "Don't worry, my lady.. My villa is on the outskirts of the city in the vineyards of Tuscany. Look around, and as far as your eyes can see are the grapes at the heart of the Italian wine industry. I don't have the time nor inclination to keep up to all the skills one needs to develop raising a quality product, so Mario and his family look after it all."

Margaret wrinkled her brow. "Who is Mario if you don't mind me asking?"

Fredrico shook his head.. "It's rather complicated but I always think of Mario as a cousin. He's more than that. You could say he was one of my father's indiscretions from long ago." Fredrico added, "Mario is my half brother. My father kept a mistress before the war and after Germany was defeated, she left Italy with a high ranking German officer and abandoned Mario. The poor little kid was left on our doorstep with a letter for my father pinned to his jacket and my mother was enraged, but took care of him in spite of her anger and raised him as a member of the family. Mario married a local girl, Maria and when my father died he left the estate to me and the vineyards to Mario. So it has worked out very well and Mario's family live in the bottom floor of my house." He turned the car onto a narrow lane, lined with slender cypress trees and Margaret could see in the distance a large yellow brick three storey house.

The Tuscan sun shone brightly and she almost gasped at the scene of the pale green leaves on the vines where tiny white blossoms added a surreal touch to the picture, and stretching toward the horizon the vineyard seemed pink. Approaching the house, she said, "It looks golden. Near the Coliseum we saw a sign saying Nero's Golden House but there was nothing like this around."

Fredrico smiled. "I'm not as wealthy as Nero was, but his house is underground that little hill in the park."

Margaret turned to him and asked, "Is this your house we are coming to?" When Fredrico nodded with a smile, she turned in the seat to face him and asked, "What do you do for a living?"

"I am a film director or a producer. Italy is famous for its films and film stars."

Margaret searched her memory." Then you must know Sophia Loren and her husband, Carlo Ponti."

"He's one of my best friends. Poor old Carlo. He's not in the best of health. I must invite them to the villa this summer when his boys are finished the school term. They love Tuscany. Mario keeps a few donkeys for the children to ride. His sons often ride out to the vineyard where Mario is working and they bring a hot lunch and some cold wine for their papa." He parked the car in the shade of the house and as Margaret stepped out she noticed a very tidy yard with scattered odds and ends hanging on the wall under the house from whence a delicious aroma wafted. Fredrico led her on a terra cotta tiled path toward the courtyard at the front of the house and as they climbed a curved stairway to the front door, Margaret gazed down upon a splashing fountain in the center of the intricate pattern formed by a low growing hedge bordering a colourful rose garden. They came to the terra cotta tile of the main patio where several huge yellow umbrellas shaded circular white tables A round woman with an ample white apron opened the door and smiled as she greeted Signor Scalise.

He turned to bring Margaret forward and introduced her to Maria as a friend of Signor Longfellow.. Maria held the door open and stepped backward in deference to Margaret's entrance into a spacious foyer where sunlight streaming through the large windows turned a polished wooden floor, golden. A massive crystal chandelier hung over a beige carpeted spiral stair case where several gilt framed masterpieces hung on the walls. Margaret turned to Fredrico and said, "I've never seen a more beautiful home. Thank you for allowing me to come here.. I've read about Italy and Tuscany, but never dreamed I would ever get to see it like this.. I wish Doug could have come too." Fredrico patted her arm and said "Douglas will be more than welcome whenever he is well enough to travel. Now, let's go down to the office and take care of your business."

The office was located to the rear of the house and consisted of dark cedar bookshelves and a large desk where a diminutive, dark haired, olive skinned young woman was busy at a bank of computers. She looked up from her work as Fredrico introduced her as Tina, Mario's and Maria's daughter., Christina. He gave her the cards bearing the information for Doug's health insurance and told her he would take the call in his office. He indicated to Margaret that she should join him, and she followed him into a large sunny room where a long table lay, covered with papers The telephone rang and the efficient Christina had established contact with the insurance company. Margaret sat down in a leather covered swivel chair to listen while Fredrico answered and explained the situation to the person on the other end of the line. He smiled when he hung up and said, "The director knew all about it because the morning news reported how a Canadian tourist had accidentally discovered the oldest tomb in Italy, and from the description of the injuries, he was expecting our call."

Margaret crossed her legs and said, "I guess we can thank Gordon Jenson for all the publicity. I wonder if Canada is transmitting the same information I must try to reach Doug's children soon"

Fredrico moved the telephone closer to her across the desk. "Go out to Christina and give her their telephone numbers and she will put the calls through in here."

Margaret glanced at her watch, "What time do you suppose it is in Toronto and Nairobi?"

Fredrico squinted at the wall clock and took out his pen to make some rough calculations. "I'd say it's about six in the morning in Toronto, and about the same as here in Nairobi."

Margaret stood up and opened her purse. "I can probably reach Anne before she starts the morning shift at the hospital and I'll call Michael's office at the UN."

Tina quickly wrote down the information, and before Margaret took her seat again in the office, the phone rang, and halfway across the world, a sleepy doctor picked up her telephone to the voice of her step mother who described the events of yesterday and said that Doug would be calling her as soon as he was well enough to leave the hospital. Assured of her father's condition, she called to Dick to turn on the television immediately for the morning world report.

Michael's secretary didn't know what to make of the call, so Margaret spoke to her instead and told her to tell Michael to call his sister and watch the news on television this evening and his father would call him at home on Sunday,

Fredrico was sitting on his chair behind the desk with his hands cupping his head, the chair tilted back with his shiny shoes on the wide window sill. He reached to the humidor on the corner of the desk, lit a cigar. The smoke curled around his head and he resumed his position, turning toward Margaret, he said, "I've been thinking about all this and have pretty well decided this story would make a good introduction to a project we are thinking of doing on the Etruscans."

He took his shoes off the desk and sat up straight to make some quick notations on a paper pad. He spoke to Tina on the inter-com telling her to advise her mother he and his guest would eat lunch on the patio. As he rose, Margaret realised that as the guest she should prepare to leave and asked, "Fredrico, I suppose your villa has a rest room." He answered quickly, "Of course, my dear lady. Come this way." He accompanied her into the hallway and opened another gilt trimmed door and said, "I will wait for you at the front door after I change my clothes. I've worn this suit for two days!"

Entering the rest room, Margaret was not surprised by the opulence before her. Mirrors covered the walls from the marble floors to the ceiling. The basin resembled a seashell with golden faucets. Thick pink towels and face cloths were arranged in another seashell on the pink veined marble counter. The stool did not sit on the floor but projected from the marble covered wall as did the bidet. Almost reluctant to disturb the pristine beauty, Margaret dried her hands on a tissue from her handbag and deposited it back into her purse and patted a stray hair before emerging to see Fredrico, wearing a fresh, short sleeved shirt and cream coloured slacks, examining the window sill behind a golden brocade drape. She smiled brightly and asked "How long have you lived in this house Fredrico?"

He turned to open the door.. "I've lived here all my life. My grandfather built it and planted the vineyard.. Some of our family have always lived in this house even during the war. Because of my father's opposition to the Fascists, we had to flee to the mountains in Lombardy, but not for long, until the Allies liberated Italy and the populace shot and hung the dictator by his heels in the center of Rome. The balcony is still there on the Venetian Piazza."

Margaret nodded. "We saw that place on our tour of the city."

Fredrico continued, "When we came home some of our possessions had been looted, but the most important thing remained …. the vineyard. After much work we repaired the winery buildings and life went on until my father and I had a falling out and I left Siena for the south and that's when I went into the film business. I worked for several years at Victory Studio. learning to be a camera operator, and then I got a big break. The boss at Victory had decided to do a picture with Rossellini. His work was reviewed fairly well in Italy and later in Europe. Rossellini became arrogant and signed the American film star, Ingrid Bergman to do Stromboli, and Ozzie, my boss, sent me to the set to work with Rossellini. He was impossible to work with because he made up the story as we went along because he said he wanted the characters to appear natural and they never saw a finished script. Miss Bergman was desperate and she almost returned to America where directors knew how to make films. But Rossellini knew how to persuade her to stay. So she did and married him even though he was a scoundrel and brought her much unhappiness. So I learned some things from Rossellini, how not to make a film and to stay away from women." As Fredrico finished speaking, he pulled out a white wrought iron chair covered with a yellow cushion and seated Margaret at the table under an umbrella overlooking the rose garden. She noticed the colourful dinnerware on a white lace place mat and a round matching orange teapot. She smiled at Fredrico and said "This is wonderful ….. just what I need. Would you like a cup of tea?" He handed his cup and saucer to her as Maria arrived bearing a bowl of pasta. She returned later with a crystal bowl of green salad and a dish of butter and a platter of rolls wrapped in a colourful cloth..

Frederico sighed and said, "Ah home, sweet home. I'm sorry Philip will be in hospital another month He should be here in the beauty of Tuscany during spring. Doctor Matera also told me he wants to have a consultation on Philip's injuries." Margaret swallowed her tea and asked, "Did he say why? It must have been serious. To call in a specialist for a broken leg seems rather odd."

Frederico sipped his tea. "It is because he has noticed a rash on his thighs and a lump in his groin. I feel afraid, like something ominous is about to happen. I myself have the same symptoms."

Noting the tone of his voice changing, she reached out to touch his hand." Don't be afraid, Fredrico. We will pray for Philip.. I know God answers prayer."

Fredrico's voice changed."I've given up on God. When my father died of a heart attack, I asked the priest to consecrate a plot of ground by the vineyard for my father's grave. He refused unless we paid him money. My friend Ozzie became enraged and the priest threatened to report us to the archbishop because he said we were homosexuals and there was no place in the church for us! So what do I care about what God thinks!"

Stunned by his outburst, Margaret remained silent praying for the words she felt God wanted her to say. "Fredrico, the God, that Doug and I worship is a forgiving, loving God who sent his Son Jesus Christ to die for all of our sins, and when we confess that we are sinners, we can receive Him as our Saviour and live with Him as our Lord."

Fredrico narrowed his eyes and added, "So you are saying homosexuals are sinners?"

Margaret breathed deeply, waiting for inspiration from on high. "Fredrico, I believe the Bible is the Word of God, and if you take the time to read it, you will discover God has a great deal to say about homosexuality in the Old Testament, especially in the account of Sodom and Gomorrah."

"Aha!" Fredrico exclaimed. "You will notice that Jesus never said anything about homosexuality in the New Testament. I've heard all the arguments"

Help me Margaret prayed silently. Pausing she said, "Well you must understand that Jesus spoke most of the time to Jews who were very aware of what their law said about it, and when you read the epistles of St. Paul, you find his condemnation of the practice in his writings to the Gentile world where homosexuality was rampant." She reached out to touch Fredrico's arm, "I don't want to seem harsh and judgmental but I know God wants me to speak the truth and tell you Jesus Christ came into the world to save sinners and, as St. Paul said, 'I was *one of the worst until I came to the truth.*'"

"So what should I do? Dump Philip? I love him with all of my heart. I can't turn away from him now when he needs me so much."

Margaret said softly, "Fredrico, you need to pray and make your peace with God, and His Holy Spirit will come to you and live in you and show you what to do. Have you heard the phrase,' Born Again'? When you ask Jesus Christ to save you, He will make you a new person and you will live a new life. All your old life will pass away and you will be surprised what the Lord will do for you. Once you are 'born again' as a child of God you will never have to be afraid of what God will do. It will always be for your own good because he loves you so much that he allowed His own precious Son to take the guilty verdict upon Himself, the guilt of your sins."

Margaret looked into Fredrico's eyes. "I'm going to pray for you that you will take a step toward your Saviour." She bowed her head, sensitive to the struggle, which was happening within her companion, praying that the powers of darkness holding him fast would be vanquished by the angels of light.

Fredrico's head remained bowed for a long time until he finally said, "So what do I do now?"

Margaret squeezed his arm and replied, "Now I think we should go shopping for a Bible, or do you already have one?"

"In the house, there may be one my father used to have. He may have read it because he was so enraged when he found Alphonse and myself out in the vineyard. He whipped us with his riding crop and ordered us to leave his sight immediately.! Poor Alphonse had nowhere to go and no money, nor a job to pay for a home, but I knew where I would go ... to Rome to make films. I had saved a little money and had no experience except taking pictures with a little camera, and Alphonse and I went our separate ways. Arriving in Rome all alone, I went to Victory studios and applied for a job. Ozzie recognized my plight and took me home with him and started me on my way to fame and fortune. My father died shortly and Alphonse came back to Rome to find me and told me about my father.. Ozzie didn't want me to go anywhere with Alphonse so he insisted on returning to Siena with me. When he saw my inheritance, his love for Tuscany overcame his good sense and he insisted on being allowed to renovate the house with his own money because the house had suffered from the lack of repairs and the vandalism while we had fled to Lombardy during the war. With his impeccable artist's eye and the top designers at the studio he transformed the place into the thing of beauty that it is today. It still needs a great deal of care that I don't expect Maria to give to it, so a cleaning staff from Siena make a weekly visit. And now, Margaret, I would like to take you on a tour of the upper floors so you can see how the poor people of Tuscany live."

Mararet folded her table napkin and rose to follow Fredrico into the house. As they mounted the spiral staircase she paused to look at the paintings hanging on the wall. She gazed at one of sailing ships engaged in battle, the colours muted and the figures precise, she asked, "Fredrico? Is this a Turner?" He stopped and gazed at her in surprise. "Are you familiar with old paintings?"

She shook her head and replied, "Not at all. When I lived in Toronto I used to go to the art gallery whenever I could get away, and once there was an exhibition of Turners. I loved it. I had no idea he was such a prolific artist." She put on her reading glasses to search the corner of the canvas for the name of the artist and turned away "Jean Paul Claudet?" she asked. "I've never heard of him."

Fredrico smiled. "He's the most famous copyist in the art world. Ozzie discovered him in Paris and commissioned him to paint his hero's flagship. Jean Paul spent a long time in the Tate Gallery in London copying the oil "The Battle of Trafalgar." What you are looking at now, is what Jean Paul remembered. Jean Paul Claudet is apsuedonym for his Italian name, Benito Francari. He changed it so he would be accepted by the Parisian community of artists. The name Benito caused a lot of hostility. Ozzie could have sent him to Portsmouth harbour in England to see the Victory as it is today. But, looking at this, you get a sense of all the drama of that sea battle when Admiral, Lord Horatio Nelson defeated the navies of Spain and France. That dealt a staggering blow to Napoleon's aspirations for world domination. Ozzie's hero was fatally wounded in that battle and brought home to England in a barrel of white wine to preserve his body for a state funeral at St. Paul's Cathedral."

Margaret examined the details of the ship carefully. "Is it really possible to see this ship today? It is so beautiful. I know Doug would love to see it. We hadn't planned to go to England on our tour. But I'm convinced that we must see this too."

Fredrico laughed. "Now you sound like Ozzie. He would love to talk to you and tell you all about the Napoleonic wars. History was his hobby and made him rich."

Margaret hesitated and asked, "Where is Ozzie? Doug would enjoy meeting him because he's a history teacher and loves to read anything he can get his hands on. That's why we came to Italy to learn about the Etruscans."

Fredrico rubbed his chin. "I'm sorry to tell you …. My dear Ozzie is dead. He passed away ten years ago and I buried him in a grave beside my father in the vineyard because both of them loved this land so much. I know my father wouldn't appreciate it because Ozzie's and my relationship wasn't what he wanted but Ozzie spent much of his fortune repairing our family home. He begged me to allow him to die here among the hills of Tuscany, so he spent his last days lying in the sunshine on the front piazza listening to the activities of harvest in the vineyard and watching Antonio working in the rose garden."

Margaret said, "I'm sorry, Fredrico He sounds like a very interesting man. And I'm curious. You said his knowledge of history made him rich and I wonder how.. History hasn't made Doug rich, but it has provided a good living for him and he's happy with that."

Fredrico took her elbow and guided her up the remaining stairway to a long dark green carpeted hallway which ended with a small, oval, stained glass window. He opened a wide door to show her a large bedroom with an expanse of glass overlooking the vineyard. A pale blue duvet covered a huge bed in the center of the room. Matching blue walls and a thick mushroom carpet added an air of tranquility to the room. "This is my bedroom," Fredrico said, "And through here is Philip's room.." They crossed the room to a gleaming marble tile bathroom with a sunken jacuzzi in one corner and a pebbled glass shower stall in the opposite corner with thick white and navy towels piled on a marble bench and navy soap dishes and shaving mugs on the counter beside two basins.

Margaret said, "I'm so impressed by the decor of this house. The hallway with the dark green carpet and the burgundy stripe on the gold flecked wall paper is so elegant. Did you choose it, Fredrico?"

"No," he said slowly. "The set designers at Victory chose all the furnishings. Ozzie wanted nothing but the best. After he died, I took over his bedroom and this was mine where Philip sleeps now. He opened the door into another large room with an equal expanse of glass overlooking the vineyard. The same mushroom carpet covered the floor. The walls were painted the mushroom shade and the furnishings, a chaise longue and the duvet on the huge bed were a deep chocolate brown as were the lampshades on the bedside tables. Fredrico said," The guest rooms are next with separate bathrooms. "Opening the door into the hall where sunlight streamed through the stained glass window, and as Margaret gazed in wonder, Fredrico led her through another doorway across the hall. "This was one of Ozzie's creations," he said. She wondered for a moment until Fredrico reached for a light switch inside the door.

"A movie theatre!" she gasped as she gazed at rows of padded seats facing a large screen at one end of the huge room. "I've never seen such a thing. "My goodness! There are so many seats. How many people does it accommodate?"

"As many as we need, by the time we get the production staff in here. You see, Margaret we don't make films for the commercial theatres. This isn't Hollywood, Italian style, because there are too many problems with the star system and outrageous contracts. Ozzie learned that with Rossellini and he took a long look at the industry and set a different course. Television was coming into its own and there was a shortage of good films. So Ozzie, with his love of history decided Italy was perfectly situated to make documentaries about the people and places who have earned a share in the spotlight on the world stage. It has become very successful. We use students at the leading universities to do the research and the property department has its problems locating or fabricating old chariots and armour. Costumes are very important to add to the authenticity of the films We have an extensive public relations department to persuade governments to allow us beyond their borders to film special sites or inside museums. To do a piece on Marco Polo or Genghis Khan we must get inside China, and once there, we try to film a piece on the Great Wall or the terra cotta army. Most countries have found we increase their tourist trade. Now I must leave you to meet with Mario.".

Descending the curved staircase into the golden foyer, Margaret said, "I would love to see the rest of the house. Would you mind if I continued on?"

"Not at all", Fredrico replied.. "You will find some lovely paintings in the salon."

Margaret walked slowly into a large golden room where a white marble fireplace and a mantle with exquisite Faberge eggs occupied the opposite wall. A round marble coffee table was surrounded by a group of mahogany Chippendale chairs, the seats covered in gold brocade. Other occasional chairs were grouped about the picture window overlooking the front piazza and rose garden.. A tall wine cabinet stood at the opposite end of the room beside a heavy, carved wooden door, and Margaret roamed about the room squinting to observe the signatures on a group of gilt framed oil paintings" Cezanne," she murmured, gazing at the still life picture of apples and the next, onions and a wine bottle and oddly enough a group of skulls. Wondering, she shook her head, convinced she needed an art book to help her understand the artist and why such a simple picture should be considered as a work of art. Turning to another grouping beside the fireplace, she discovered a plaque stating Gauguin's two women on a beach and beside it another plaque stating Gauguin's two women harvesting in Brittany.. She smiled, wondering at Gauguin's fondness for painting two women wherever he happened to be. On the other side of the fireplace she saw two wonderful pictures labelled as the work of Renoir, the Boating Party Lunch, full of life and colour. Margaret thought she could gaze at it for a very long time, comparing the facial expressions and wondering about the dynamics of the group. Beside it, she found a lovely picture of a sweet little girl with a watering can and thought Renoir painted it symbolically with a flagstone path leading away from the child into her future She then decided Renoir must have painted the girl on his knees because her face was at eye level. In the corner of the painting were two signature, Renoir,/ Jean Paul Claudet. Overcome by her discovery she sat down on a gold brocade French provincial settee to drink in the beauty of the room with the pale yellow walls. The Faberge eggs on the mantel tempted a closer examination but she declined thinking she dare not touch the exquisite jewelled objects lest a careless move might damage them. She reasoned she would wait for Fredrico before touching them. Noticing the carvings on the door beside the wine cabinet, she rose to observe the crystal goblets and decanters on the various shelves and opened the heavy door into a large mahogany paneled room The ceiling was ornately carved in clusters of grapes. A long mahogany table stretched the length of the room with a matching side board resplendent with silver urns.. Six silver candelabra occupied the shining surface of the table spaced at intervals. Overhead were lances projecting from the high walls bearing colourful pennants, similar to the banners she had seen waving in the Piazza di Palio and Fredrico had told her they represented the seventeen electoral wards of Sienna. The late afternoon sun shone through the golden glassed gothic windows in the wall above another side board where china and glassware was stored. Margaret walked slowly the length of the table, her hand trailing across the carved backs of the dinner chairs. She raised her eyes to study the canopies overhead, scarlet, yellow, bright green and royal blue with separate designs of a she-wolf, goose, dragon, panther, eagle, unicorn, ram, giraffe, forest and othersr. All were emblems of the military companies hired to defend Siena's fiercely earned independence from Florence and other nearby city states. Over the centuries, the wards were held together by emotions and devotions and marriages, baptisms….. Deaths and church holidays were all occasions for feasting and celebrations.. When Margaret opened the door at the end of the dining room, she found Fredrico drinking a glass of water at a sink. He smiled, "Would you like a drink?" he asked handing a crystal glass to her.. "So how do you like the house? Is it too formal?"

Margaret grinned. "I don't think it's too formal if you are entertaining heads of state. Frankly, I've never seen such luxury. I was afraid to touch the Faberge eggs on the mantel. The designers at Victory studios must have had a wonderful time working on this house. Are you sure you're not as rich as Nero? His golden house could never be as lovely as yours. Of course he didn't have the art by

Cezanne, Gauguin and Renoir to add a touch of class to his palace. I wonder if he had a rose garden."

Fredrico averted his eyes. "He had a garden, according to the historians of the time. He tied Christians to stakes, poured oil over them and set them afire to illuminate the gardens for his guests to enjoy their wine, women and song. Well, Margaret, I suppose we had better get on our way. Your husband and Philip will be wondering where we are. Although Philip knows how long the journey to the house takes with the traffic this time of day."

Fredrico led her down a flight of stairs where she could hear the sounds from Maria's kitchen and an Italian tenor singing on a stereo system. Fredrico turned to her to say, "Isn't that aroma heavenly? We won't get anything like that for dinner in Siena."

Margaret glanced up the staircase. "Surely, Maria doesn't carry all the food up these stairs when you eat dinner in the dining room?"

"Surely not," Fredrico replied "She uses the elevator, what I think you call it, a dumb waiter. It goes from her kitchen to a closet in the pantry. The dinner plates come down to the kitchen to be washed." He opened a door which led outside to the parked Fiat. She watched Fredrico as he left the yard with a toot of the horn and drove confidently as his manicured hands gripped the steering wheel while the car turned onto the autostrada. The traffic became heavy as they reached the perimeter of the city. Margaret drew a relaxed sigh as Fredrico's skills in navigation became more apparent in the narrow streets of Siena. He wore his cream coloured fedora tilted forward to shut out the evening sunshine, They reached the parking lot of the hospital and the Fiat stopped beside a silver grey Bentley where a grey liveried chauffeur stood at attention as they approached. "Carlo," Fredrico said. "You had better get some supper because I think we will be returning to Tarquinia this evening. I will have to wait and see if Signora Parker's husband is discharged, and then we will go immediately. I will return," He glanced at his wrist watch, "at seven thirty." He adjusted the sleeve on his navy blue linen sport jacket with shiny silver buttons.

Chapter Four

MARGARET SOON LEARNED the difficulties associated with someone with celebrity status. As they entered the doors of the emergency department, they were immediately surrounded by newspaper reporters and photographers. Signor Scalise was bombarded with questions about his partner Philip Longfellow and his Canadian friend Signor Parker. And then, they turned to Margaret and asked permission to take her photo, and asked what she thought of her husband's relationship with Signor Longfellow. Completely bewildered, she stammered, "Relationship? There is no relationship. They are just friends...."

Fredrico came to her rescue. "Excusa. Signora Parker is very tired. We have an appointment to see the doctor who is attending to them." Taking Margaret's elbow, he ushered her through a swinging door and enquired of the first nurse they saw where they could find the elevator to take them to the third floor. Unaccosted, they reached their destination where sounds of laughter and merriment emanated from Philip's room. Fredrico asked the whereabouts of Dr. Matera. The nurse glanced at the clock and told them Dr.. Matera had left for the day.. She came close to Fredrico and said, "I wish you could do something about Philip's visitors. They are so rowdy we've already had to move Mr. Parker from the room."

Margaret asked quickly. "Where have you put Mr. Parker?"

The nurse asked, "You are Mrs. Parker?"

"Yes. Where did you put Mr. Parker?"

The nurse came to her side. "He is in the solarium. I will show you." She led Margaret to a large room at the end of the corridor where a semi circle of windows overlooked the skyline of Sienna, dark against the setting sun across the Tuscan hills. Doug sat slumped in the old wooden wheelchair. His face lighted as Margaret stooped to kiss his cheek. "How are you, darling? You look so tired."

He smiled at her. "I've missed you so much. Philip's friends came in to see him and they are so phony. I feel sick just thinking about it. It was dahling this and dahling that until I couldn't stand to listen to them any longer so I asked the nurse to take me away. She brought me here which isn't exactly the place to spend an afternoon with one old fellow who snored all the time he was here. I could hear the laughter in Philip's room and almost wished I was back there. Before you came, I was considering getting out of this contraption and leaving the hospital. But I didn't have any place to go so that didn't seem like a very good idea. So tell me, what you have been doing all day.?"

"I've been seeing the sights of Siena and you'll never guess who I met today outside the hospital. I came across a tour bus of Canadians. Do you remember I told you about seeing my former pastor on the train who introduced me to Peter Spencer the friend of Harry at St. Jude's. I knew Jim Pearson's wife quite well. We used to play bridge at the church. Poor Bridget fell down outside their hotel and broke both wrists. She was here in the emergency room being treated by our Doctor Matera. Isn't it a small world! Afterwards, Fredrico came along and drove us up the hill to the Duomo where her tour was scheduled. After that, Fredrico drove me out to his house in the wine country. I wish you could have seen it, dahling. It is really beautiful. Perhaps someday? Fredrico is quite a man. He's a film producer here in Rome. He knows Sophia Loren and her husband very well. He's met Ingrid Bergman too and from the looks of his house, he's very wealthy and has a fabulous art collection.."

Doug rubbed his chin. "Let's go down to the nursing station and see when I can get out of here. It will cost a fortune to take a cab back to the Lido at Tarquinia, but it will be worth it." Margaret pushed him back through the corridor and spoke to the nurse about Doug's discharge. Fredrico came along and said, "Apparently, Dr. Matera has requested a therapist see you and place your arm in a sling and a shoulder brace. "The nurse nodded in agreement. While they were speaking, Philip's two friends approached and told Fredrico they would be in touch with him about Philip's condition. Margaret was astonished to see the one friend wearing a bright lemon yellow three piece suit while the other was garbed in a raspberry colour three piece suit. They looked fondly at Fredrico who suggested to the Parkers that they come with him to say goodnight to Philip. Margaret was shocked to see Philip looking so pale and listless. They beat a hasty retreat leaving Fredrico holding Philip's hand and kissing his brow. The nurse assisted Gino, the therapist, who was waiting at Doug's bedside and showed Margaret how to put the shoulder brace on Doug. He winced as the brace was drawn slightly tighter and Gino explained how the brace was to provide enough tension to keep the bone ends in alignment. He assisted Margaret in dressing Doug for the return home and Fredrico arrived to explain that he had contacted the chauffer and he would be waiting at the emergency room door.. The nurse provided them with a folding wheelchair and accompanied them to the lower floor of the hospital where a few reporters had gathered to take pictures of the celebrity tourist leaving the hospital. He waved to them with a thumbs up.

Chapter Five

DUSK WAS SETTLING across the hills of Tuscany as the Parkers and Fredrico with Carlo at the wheel left the hospital parking lot in the comfort and warmth of the Bentley. Doug's new wheelchair had been folded into the spacious trunk as its occupant had slid gingerly onto the back seat while Margaret entered the car from the opposite door and sighed as she reached for his hand. Fredrico sat in the front passenger seat and turned to check on the comfort of his new friends. Carlo navigated through the traffic congestion of the evening in Siena. He leaned toward his employer and said, "Sophie took a message for you from the director of the clinic in Lucerne, late this afternoon." Fredrico opened the glove compartment and retrieved a leather bound address notebook.. Glancing outside at the sky, he rolled down his window, dialed a number and spoke quickly in Italian into his cell phone. Frowning, he said quietly, "Jean Paul has been transferred to a hospital in Paris."

Carlo asked slowly, "What does this mean?"

Fredrico turned to the driver."The director explained that his sputum tests were negative so they investigated his diagnosis of tuberculosis and have changed his diagnosis to pneumocystitis carinii."

Carlo asked again, "And what does that mean?"

Frederico rubbed his temples. "It means Jean Paul is very ill with a tumour in his chest and they have transferred him to a clinic in Paris which treats cases of advanced A ID S."

Margaret and Doug looked at each other with questioning eyes. Fredrico turned to look at them steadily. "Suddenly now, I'm very afraid for his life." With glazed eyes he said, "When I get home, I'm going to make a lot of telephone calls, even though it's very late in the evening."

The car sped smoothly along the autostrada as the passengers in the rear seat watched twinkling lights of hamlets in the distant hills. Very quickly they came to the off ramp for Tarquinia. Carlo turned slowly onto the road leading to the beach. Several illuminated signs for the Hotel Lido shone on the marshy fields. As Carlo pulled underneath the spreading umbrella pines around the parking lot, Fredrico said, "Doug, if you remain in the car, we will go in with Margaret to complete the checking out process. If you don't mind we will lock the doors to protect you."

Doug smiled. "A good idea. I don't want to be mugged in a parking lot. I see our rental car is still here just where we left it. It seems like eons ago. So much has happened."

Margaret kissed his cheek as she gathered her purse to follow Carlo and Fredrico to the side entrance of the hotel, the rooms above, in darkness..

The sleepy desk clerk looked at them as though they were invading the premises. Fredrico explained the reason for the abbreviated tenure. Margaret signed the receipt for the credit card and took the elevator with Carlo to their room. She quickly filled their suitcases with the contents of the closets and the toiletries from the bathroom. Carlo watched her swift efficiency and carried the luggage to the elevator as Margaret kneeled to check under the bed and found Doug's long lost brown sock which she stuffed into her purse. Fredrico was waiting in the lobby and helped Carlo carry the bags to the car to squeeze them in around the wheelchair.

Doug raised his eyebrows. "All taken care of? Did you get everything?"

She opened her purse and dangled the sock. "Under the bed."

"Oh good," he said." I wondered where that had gone. Now I won't have to wear the black socks."

Carlo swung the car out onto the street of the promenade and continued on to a cordoned White Palace, where a guard house stood at the entrance to a ground level parking garage. Carlo drove to the far end and parked the car in front of a group of elevators. Fredrico produced a key and the shining steel doors opened. Margaret came around to help Doug out of the limousine to sit in the wheelchair as Carlo loaded the luggage onto a carpeted trolley. The elevator whirred to the penthouse on the eighth floor where the doors opened into a square foyer decorated in shades of aqua and peach with several paintings and lighted sconces on the walls. A tall slender woman with white hair appeared immediately and smiled as Carlo reached for her hand. After the customary introductions, Fredrico said, "If you come this way we will show you to your room.," They followed Sophie along a corridor to a large room with glass doors leading to a balcony overlooking the Tyrrhenian Sea. The room was tastefully decorated in tones of aqua and peach with a fluffy counterpane on a huge bed with a white headboard and bedside tables. An aqua coloured chaise longue and a white leather tub chair were arranged in front of a television set. A painting on the wall drew Margaret's attention and she walked over to look at it more closely while Doug rose from the wheelchair to sit in the chair. Frederico said, "I trust you will be quite comfortable here. If you should need more pillows, Douglas, Sophie will get you several from Philip's room".

Margaret turned and asked, "Another of Jean Paul?"

"Yes. It's a Raphael. The original hangs in the National Gallery in Vienna. It is titled' The Visit'. The woman seated is Mary of Nazareth and of course, the baby on her lap is the Christ child. The toddler holding out a toy to the baby is John the Baptist and the other woman watching so carefully is John's mother, Elizabeth."

"It's delightful," Margaret said. "Look at it, Doug. It's so full of joy. Look at the smile on Jesus' face."

Fredrico cleared his throat. "I am going to leave you now for a while. Will you come along to the lounge for some refreshments?" Sophie smiled and excused herself as Doug decided to walk about and investigate the balcony. The Parkers found their way along the corridor to another large room with open doors to a balcony. Sophie entered, wheeling an elaborate silver tea service. She lifted the tray onto a glass topped table in front of a long white leather settee.. Other leather chairs were grouped about the room in front of a large screen television set. Margaret glanced about the room to see what paintings were there. She was surprised to see several pastel Picassos with their misfit heads and body parts. which almost blended into the aqua and peach walls. She said, "Who was it said, and I quote, 'Abstract art? A product *of* the *untalented*, sold *by the unprincipled to the utterly bewildered.*'? I'm not suggesting Fredrico is bewildered, but I much prefer the water lillies of Manet. Sophie carried a tray of sandwiches and canapes to the coffee table. Fredrico arrived and asked Margaret to pour the tea…She smiled and sat down wondering if she could lift the heavy silver teapot and balance the delicate china cup and saucer at the same time. She remembered that Fredrico drank his tea with milk so she offered him the first cup, poured another for Doug and carried it to him where he sat in a comfortable straight backed chair. Fredrico brought the plate of sandwiches over to the occasional table beside Doug who chose a pastry wrapped sausage. As he bit into the hot canape, he said "Wow! This is delicious. I've never tasted anything as good as this except Margaret's pot roast"

Margaret sipped her tea and crossed the room to sample the tray of delights. She bit into a pastry wrapped mushroom. "Is this a truffle?" she asked Sophie who had just entered the room with a silver pot of hot water.

"Yes. Master Philip loves them. They are his favourite snack."

"I'm not surprised, "Margaret replied "I've never tasted a truffle before, but these certainly live up to their reputation." She reached for another and sat down on the settee while Fredrico explained to Doug that he could return the rental car to the airport in Rome on the morrow when he caught an afternoon flight to Paris." I must see Jean Paul before his surgery and make arrangements for Philip to be treated at St. Antoines'

Sensing his concern, Margaret said, "Doug, it's been a long day for you, and all of us, so I think it's time we should turn in for the night. "She gathered up the tea cups and the plate of sandwiches and proceeded to wheel the tea trolley out into the hall. Fredrico went ahead to lead the way into the kitchen. She searched through several drawers to find a roll of cling wrap to preserve the sandwiches and put them into a huge refrigerator. Doug and Fredrico watched as she rinsed the tea cups and tea pot, leaving them on the granite counter for Sophie to deal with in the morning.

Preparing for bed became a challenge as she carefully removed Doug's neck brace and adjusted the sling. Doug piled several pillows on his side of the bed. When Margaret finished brushing her teeth, she asked, "Do you want the doors closed or should I leave them open?"

Doug yawned and replied, "Since we're on the eighth floor, I don't think we'll have any burglars. Let's leave them open so we can hear the sounds of the waves It reminds me of sleeping on The Lady."

Turning off the lamps, Margaret snuggled close to Doug's uninjured shoulder and said a short prayer of thanks for their present situation and Fredrico's friends, Jean Paul, and Philip. She awoke to bright sunshine and since Doug was sleeping soundly, she slid out of bed and retrieved her Bible from her suitcase and sat on the chaise longue to read her daily portion of the Psalms.

Doug wakened and asked, "What's the word for today?"

She regarded him with shining eyes. "It always amazes me, as my daily reading so often fits in with what's happening to me at the time."

He furled his brow. "How do you mean?"

"Well today, It's Psalm 103 which deals with healing diseases and forgiving iniquities, Listen to these verses."

When she came to an end, Doug said, "I can't express it, but I'm so grateful to God that I'm included in all these promises."

"We can talk later, darling and then we can pray together over them. Right now, I think we should shower and get organized for the day." She went into the bathroom and gathered up a stack of towels, while Doug adjusted the water temperature and dropped his pajama pants on the floor. "It won't matter if the sling gets wet, will it?"

"Of course not," she replied "It will dry and you'll be wearing the brace." They spent a happy half hour under the warm spray with the fragrance of lemon soap as they washed each other's backs and embracing with the usual intimacy. Drying each other gently and as Doug adjusted his boxer shorts, she dried his legs and feet. Taking off her shower cap, she brushed her hair as Doug stood beside her and shaved. A tap on the bedroom door and Margaret admitted Sophie bearing a tea tray. "Signor Scalise asks that you join him for breakfast on the south patio." She indicated the location and left the room.

Margaret slipped into a cotton blouse and skirt while Doug pulled a pair of slacks from his suitcase along with a brown sock. Margaret took its mate from her purse and helped him dress his feet They carried their teacups out to the balcony and judging the east by the rising sun, Doug led her around the corner of the building to the south patio where Fredrico sat at a round table with a brightly coloured tablecloth flapping in a breeze. "Good morning, I trust you slept well."

"Like the proverbial baby," Doug replied "That bed was so comfortable."

"And the pillows," Margaret echoed." They are absolutely heavenly."

"Philip thinks so," Fredrico said. "There are several more in his room if you would like any extra to help with your shoulder, Poor Philip. I suppose they will give him sleeping medication to help him through the night, But often those drugs do not help the quality of your sleep, I get terrible dreams if I ever take them."

"I know what you mean," Doug said, "I had a horrible nightmare when I got knocked out falling into the tomb." He gazed far down the beach to where a promontory of cliffs partially obscured a huge smoke stack.

Fredrico followed his line of vision and said "That is a coal fired electrical plant that provides all the energy for Rome The coal is shipped in by freighter but there is some local coal that the Etruscans used to smelt the iron ore they brought in from Corsica and Sardinia,

On a clear day you can see the islands on the horizon, We are getting closer to summer so the heat obscures the horizon,"

"You have a lovely home here, Fredrico," Doug said,

"Philip and I find it very comfortable, When we first moved to Tarquinia, because of the antiquities, the housing market was very limited, A wind surfing competition brought hordes of people to the beach. Overnight, the place changed and Roman developers moved in with condominiums planned all along the coast. Philip and I were lucky to get our choice with this one. We like the freedom of the open beach at the end of the road and no building next door so our balconies are private and we don't have strangers peering at us."

"Have you heard from Dr Matera?" Margaret asked.

"Yes," Fredrico replied "He's making arrangements for Philip to fly out of Milan by air ambulance to Paris to St Antoines."

"That's wonderful," Margaret said. "Now you can be together with Jean Paul and Philip."

"Yes", Fredrico replied. "And I am going to join them too.."

She lay her hand on his arm. "Is there any change this morning?"

"No",. The spots and lump are still there. So I will have a better idea what's happening when I reach Paris this afternoon."

She frowned.

"Don't worry." he said "I'm leaving Sophie and Carl to take care of you. After you have seen the sights in Italy, perhaps you would care to join us in Paris?"

Margaret glanced at Doug who said, "We never included France in our itinerary, but that sounds like a great idea, don't you think so, Margaret?"

She smiled at Fredrico. "I'd love to see Paris especially Versailles because I read a story about Marie Antoinette pretending to be a shepherdess and an actress."

Doug held up his hand. "Wait a minute, Margaret. You do come up with outrageous anecdotes! Remember when you told me about Queen Elizabeth the first, being a man!"

She laughed with Fredrico who said, "I've heard that same story, Doug."

Doug shook his head.. "I'm glad you two don't write the text books."

Fredrico said, "It's absolutely true. When you are in Paris, I'll take you to the little hamlet where she lived and tended her sheep which were heavily perfumed by the way. And we'll go to the little theater where she performed in amusing French farces. The poor woman was desperate to escape her real life. Born to a royal cradle in Austria, traded into a loveless marriage, and an outsider in a court of vicious gossip and intrigue. She suffered a miscarriage and afterward, was constantly pressured to produce an heir. When you come to Paris, I'll make arrangements for you to stay with Hubert the butler at Jean Paul's house near Versailles."

"Fredrico," Margaret began, "I can't begin to thank you for all you are doing to take care of Doug and me."

"Margaret," he replied, "You must understand I am so grateful to you and Doug for saving my dear Philip's life. If it weren't for you two, he would have bled to death in the hills of Volterra."

Sophie came to the table with a fresh pot of coffee. "There is a telephone call for you, Signor."

Fredrico excused himself and left the table immediately.. He returned shortly, followed by Sophie bearing a covered dish. He took his seat at the table and lifted the lid. "Ahhh, scrambled eggs." Serving himself, he passed the dish to Doug. Sophie returned with a plate of sausage and a rack of unbuttered toast. They helped themselves to the condiments on a tray on the center of the table, marmalade, tomato sauce and thick cream for the coffee.

Margaret has been telling me about your vocation, Fredrico," Doug said. "It sounds like a very interesting business."

"It is," Fredrico replied. "This poor boy from the vineyards has travelled the world and met some very interesting people. My benefactor, Ozzie, was like a father to me and taught me everything I know. Ozzie was not a father but my lover when I was young with no education. He gave me a deep love for history, which I understand you share too, Douglas. If there is any way I can help you broaden your knowledge, I will be happy to do so."

Doug swallowed his coffee. "I don't know what to say, Fredrico, but you seem so capable to know exactly what you are doing and where you are going."

"I have to," Fredrico replied. "I am the C E O of Victory Film Studios here in Rome and I have to know what is going on in our world and what has happened. I never knew what lay ahead for me when Ozzie sent me to Paris to do a story on Armand Hammer, the American oil tycoon, and his involvement with Jean Paul Claudet"

Doug turned to him to ask, "Will you tell us about it? I've heard of Armand Hammer, the baking soda maker, the Hooker Chemical company and the Love Canal tragedy?"

Fredrico leaned back in his chair and took a cigar from the pocket of his jacket hanging over the back of his chair "Do you mind if I smoke?"

"Of course not," they said in unison.

He struck a match on the sole of his shoe and began," Armand Hammer was born at the turn of the century to a Russian immigrant doctor in New York City. His father was an entrepreneur who began a career of making potions and ointments and even drugs for the poor. His mother, Mama Rose thought every ailment could be cured by a dose of soda bicarbonate and an enema. Young Armand was admitted to Columbia University to study medicine and, due to family circumstances, ended up running his father's company very successfully, while carrying on with his studies at Columbia. That year, he earned his first million dollars. And, because of his name, he entered into negotiations with the company of Dwight and Church who made the baking soda, Arm and Hammer. His mother swears that she named her son after a character in a French novel by Dumas, the author who wrote the Three Musketeers. Young Hammer purchased a share of the company and contributed to its success. His father bought a yacht and hung a flag with an arm and a hammer and sickle from the stern. After Russia calmed down following the Bolshevik revolution in 1917, and a typhus epidemic, Armand Hammer went to Russia with his medical degree, thinking he could help. With Lenin running the country, Hammer saw the hardship and starvation of the general populace. He entered into negotiations trading Russian furs for American grain. It, too, turned out very well and he returned to America. The baking soda company in which he had invested was ripe for a take-over bid by Occidental Petroleum and he was able to obtain a seat on the board of directors. He returned to Russia as a good-will ambassador for the United States, Armand Hammer settled into the Russian life style. He developed a fondness for the arts and was able to amass a collection of fine art of the old masters and the new Russian artists. After Lenin's death when Joseph Stalin came to power, Hammer could not accept Stalin's brutality and resigned his ambassadorship and left for France. He watched the Nazi invasion of the Sudetenland and Poland and was truly alarmed as the Nazi troops occupied the Lowlands and turned their war machines toward France. He realized that the Nazi generals had a fondness for confiscating art from private collections and museums and galleries to send them on to Berlin. While walking along the left bank of the Seine, one day, and viewing the art, he saw a remarkable likeness of a Rembrandt. He knew it could not be the original and his curiosity drove him to inquire and this led him to a young Italian artist, Benito Francari, who because of the war and the animosity of things Italian, had changed his name to Jean Paul Claudet to avoid a confrontation with the other starving artists on the left bank. After his first meeting with Hammer, Jean Paul disappeared from the scene into the chateau, Hammer had purchased in the park among the oak trees which the squirrels from Versailles had planted by burying their acorns.

Quite happily, Jean Paul set to work on the commission given to him by his benefactor, which was to make copies of the Van Goghs and Renoirs and Monets and Gauguins which Armand Hammer had brought with him from Russia. The copies were hung on the walls of the chateau while the originals were packed away within the walls of the building. All of these palaces and mansions were built with secret passageways to facilitate the servants carrying loads of fuel to stoke the beautiful porcelain or ceramic stoves that stood in the corners of these huge rooms. Kettles of hot water were ferried from kitchen to bathrooms. Armand Hammer had all of the stoves removed from the chateau so that no servants would be traipsing through storage nooks within the walls. After Pearl Harbour, when America declared war on the Axis powers, Armand realized he was in far greater danger than his paintings, so he left Paris, travelling secretly under the protection of his protege, Benito Francari. They went to Genoa where Benito persuaded his cousin who owned a fishing trawler to cross the Ligurian Sea and head for sanctuary in Spain where Armand Hammer could get a flight from Madrid to either South or North America.

In gratitude, Hammer sent a letter to his lawyer in his Parisian office stipulating the chateau and its total contents were bequeathed to his young friend Jean Paul Claudet in event of his death or an inability to return to Paris. Apparently, he had consulted with his family who had no inclination for things Parisian. They stated a preference for the polo fields of West Palm Beach in Florida or the golf links of Palm Springs in California. Armand Hammer went on to become the chief operating officer of the company, Occidental Petroleum, and when he died, his family never questioned his decision to leave some old house in Paris to some unknown artist that they never cared to thank for saving their father's life during the war." Fredrico exhaled a plume of smoke, "And that's the story of Jean Paul Claudet."

Margaret leaned forward and said "I would like to meet this talented man."

"And so you shall. You must come to Paris soon, before it's too late." Fredrico's eyes filled with tears. "I can't bear the thought of losing Philip, too."

Much to Doug's surprise and chagrin, Margaret rose and walked around the table to cradle Fredrico's head in her arms. "We will be praying for all of you," she murmured and lightly kissed the top of his head. Doug had had enough. He rose and pushed his chair forward. "You have a lot to do today, Fredrico. We mustn't keep you any longer." He held out his hand and Fredrico shook it and laid his hand on Doug's uninjured shoulder. "Douglas, I'm afraid I have some bad news for you. Last evening in my conversation with Dr. Matera, I learned that he is concerned you may have become infected by the cut in your hand coming into contact with Philip's bloody leg."

"What!" Margaret shrieked. "Oh God! No! No. Oh Doug, What will we do?"

Fredrico put his arm around her trembling shoulders as Doug felt he wanted to draw her close but Fredrico's arm was in the way. He took her hand and said, "Margaret? You always say prayer is the answer so I think we should go and pray. Will you join us, Fredrico?" He led Margaret around the corner of the building and she had to close her eyes because of the tears and the brilliant sunshine reflecting off the surface of the sea.

Upon entering their room, they sank to their knees beside the bed. Margaret rose to answer a tap on the door and admitted Fredrico who came to kneel beside Doug. She knelt on the opposite side of the bed so she could look directly at the two men.

Fredrico rose slightly. "Please forgive me … I have interrupted your holy moment. But Signor Ricatto has called to ask you to join him to hear the report on the tomb."

Doug smiled and asked, "Margaret, will you hold my arm while I try to stand up? My knees are getting sore?

She held the sling while Doug rose and walked over to sit in the chair by the chaise longue where Fredrico had chosen to recline.

Margaret perched on the bed and said, "I met Signor Ricatto while you were about to be rescued. I may have offended him because I was afraid his portly body might collapse the tomb's ceiling as he was trying to look down the hole."

"Oh, don't worry about him," Fredrico said. "He's the curator of the museum in Volterra, and a great friend of Philip. He helped Philip get his position at the museum in Tarquinia. He asked if you could meet with him with Philip in Siena."

Margaret twisted her head to look at Doug. "So that means we have to go to Siena. Do you feel well enough to go, dear?"

Doug smiled, "I do, if Carlo could take us in that luxury car?"

Fredrico nodded. "Of course.... I still have Signor Ricatto on the 'phone. Excuse me. I'll tell him you will be there at noon."

Margaret followed Fredrico out into the corridor and Doug pursed his lips, narrowing his eyes. He heard her say "Fredrico? Could you ask Sophie to make some more of those truffles for Philip? I'm sure he would enjoy them for his lunch."

He heard Fredrico reply, "I'll ask her now. I'll say goodbye to you now, and I will see you again when I know what is happening today in Paris."

As Margaret closed the door, Doug shook his head and said, "What a man! I'm sure he's very capable running a film company. What did you say its name was?"

"Victory. Victory Studios in Rome. His former partner, Ozzie, named it after Admiral Horatio Nelson's ship that fought at the battle of Trafalgar in the Napoleonic wars. Did you know that if we went to England, we could see that ship in Portsmouth Harbour?"

"Margaret! Are you suggesting we go to Eng land too?"

"Why not?" .... "We've changed our plans before and think how much fun we've had."

Doug reached for her hand and pulled her down toward him so she sat on the chaise. as he said. "I've felt something today I haven't felt before." She frowned slightly and leaned toward him. "I was jealous of you today." Her eyes widened "The way you hugged Fredrico and kissed the top of his head...... And then he put his arm around you when he told us about this AIDS thing. I know he's attractive and rich but I don't want to lose you to him."

Margaret knelt before him and kissed his hand. "Oh darling.... You're not going to lose me to anybody. I think Fredrico is nice and I just felt sorry for him, but Doug my dearest, he's a homosexual and certainly isn't interested in me and I'm not in the least interested in him although he has been so kind to us. But now, Doug I want to pray about all that's happening." Doug had never heard anyone pray more earnestly as Margaret entered the throne room of God through the name of Jesus Christ, committing them to the loving grace of their heavenly Father, confessing that whatever came their way from

His hand was always good and a blessing, and they were content to remain in His care. She went on to intercede for Doug, Jean Paul, Philip and Fredrico and ask God to send someone to lead them to a saving knowledge of the Lord Jesus Christ.

Doug squeezed her hand and said, "Margaret, I've never heard anyone pray like you, not even Angus McKelvie."

She squeezed his hand too and said, "Maybe Angus has never been as desperate as I am. This is your life I'm trusting for, my life too, because we are one flesh, remember? bone of my bone? I couldn't live without you, darling, I wouldn't want to live without you."

They dried their eyes and dressed, preparing for the trip to Siena.

Chapter Six

W HEN CARLO RETURNED from dropping Fredrico beside the rental car in the parking lot at the Lido, the Parkers and Sophie were waiting in the shade of the front entrance of the White Palace as the silver limousine slid silently to a stop. Carlo stood at attention to open the rear doors and Sophie passed a large insulated box to him and he placed it on the passenger seat. "Carlo, please tell Mr. Philip I have lit a candle for him this morning." She stepped back from the car. Carlo closed the doors and the Bentley rolled silently away towards the marshy lowlands and the autostrada heading north to Siena. The journey passed quickly as they watched farmers ploughing the sloping fields turning over huge grey furrows of clay They were reminded of Philip telling them of landscape archaeology on the morning of the earthquake and the landslide. and wondered how many treasures were being exposed to the Tuscan sun. It seemed as only minutes had passed since they left the White Palace until they turned into the parking lot of the hospital. Doug had decided they should return the wheelchair since he felt well enough to have no further use for it. Carlo took it out of the trunk. Margaret pushed it into the emergency department and proceeded to the third floor explaining to the nurse in charge they were returning it with gratitude for its use. She inquired into the condition of Signor Longfellow and learned he was still receiving pain medication. Margaret asked, "Has lunch been served to the patients yet?"

"Sister Pagano replied "Yes. Signor Longfellow has had his tray but, when his visitor arrived, he refused to eat anymore of the food."

Margaret opened the box and gave it to her "Would you heat these a little? Do you have a micro-wave oven on the floor? They are his favourite snack."

Nurse. Pagano took the box, "Of course," she replied. "I'll make a pot of tea for him too.. Could you encourage Signor Ricatto to cut his visit shorter? Signor Longfellow is not well and should rest."

Margaret raised her eyebrows, "Philip isn't well? I understood he's being transferred to Paris this afternoon."

The nurse nodded, "That is why it is imperative that he should rest as much as possible."

"I'll see what I can do." Margaret walked slowly along the hallway and entered room 312.where Doug sat in a large lounge chair and the portly Signor Ricatto sat uncomfortably on a wooden chair by the head of the bed. The light streamed through the large window. Margaret could see quite clearly the shadows under Philip's eyes. His face looked grey and haggard against the white. sheets drawn up to his chin. His injured leg, wrapped in a tensor bandage with surgical wires protruding from the calf, lay in a sling on a metal brace and was secured by another wire through his heel.

Philip smiled weakly as she approached the bed. "Philip, I'm so glad to see you but we mustn't stay too long because you look very weary and we mustn't tire you, should we, Signor Ricatto? Do you remember me, Signor? We met at the tomb. I'm Margaret Parker. Douglas Parker is my husband." She turned slightly toward Doug and smiled as nurse Pagano entered the room, bearing a tray. "Philip, Sophie has sent you a treat." Philip endeavoured to sit up and rest on his elbows as the tray was placed on the tray table and the tea was poured.

"Ah, Sophie…. She knows the way to a man's heart."

Signor Ricatto sat up straighter to view the delicacies and Margaret was sure he licked his lips. She leaned forward, "Will you tell us now about the tomb?"

He sat back in the chair, "Ah, yes. Perhaps Signor Longfellow has told you that we know so very little about the Etruscans because they left very little of their language behind or their writings. But now, thanks to you two, we know so much more because the tomb contained two sarcophagi, inscribed with symbols which resemble the cuneiform writing on the Ebla tablet which has been deciphered many times from two thousand years before the Christ. We contacted two paleographers who were happy to be included in the find and they have ascertained that the ciphers were the same as the Ebla tablet which dates from southern Syria two thousand years B.C." He looked longingly at the truffles and Philip pushed the plate in his direction. Signor Ricatto wiped his lips with his handkerchief and Margaret was grateful Nurse Pagano had not included extra tea cups.

"And so," Margaret pushed on, "What else do you know?"

"We learned from the inscription that the people were evacuated from their home in Syria because invaders from the east attacked them and they fled to the coast of the Great Sea which would be the Mediterranean and they continued on a northerly course because previous invasions had come from the south which would have been Egypt, according to the Ebla tablet. For many seasons, they wandered along the coast, fishing and hunting game in what would have been southern Turkey. Still following the coast they came to another body of water that forced them to turn north which would have been the Dardanelles until they could see mountain tops across the water, which would have been the Straits of the Bosphorus. They remained there and built boats to transfer themselves across the water, and were met by a fierce warrior tribe. In the battle, their king was killed and the decision was made to leave for the mountains in the north. The climate was so harsh that many of their number died and they turned south to a more temperate clime. Crossing a mountain range, where they could see blue waters and two islands which would have been Corsica and Sardinia, they came down from the mountains into a land of grape vines and olive trees and fresh water. And no inhabitants. They decided to build boats to search out the islands but found them almost uninhabitable with poor soil and little vegetation but quantities of iron ore. The decision was made to settle on the mainland. After the long and arduous journey the prince regent died and was buried in the limestone sarcophagus with the bones of his father killed in battle so long ago. The second sarcophagus contained the bones and personal effects of the queen and the bones of three young children, possibly younger siblings of the prince regent The forensic labs in Rome are excited because the DNA tests show that none of these children are related to the Queen, but they are examining the bones of the prince regent and his father, the King to determine the paternity. There may have been concubines, too but we did find some gold jewellery and those beautiful burnished red vases that have also turned up in Syria."

Not wishing to prolong the visit, Margaret heard Doug ask, "Signor Ricatto? How did these primitive people know how to smelt iron from the rock or build boats to cross seas?"

The archaeologist shrugged and answered, "We don't know but we know that they did it. The Canaanites and the Philistines had experience forging weapons of iron and wheels for chariots.

<Margaret could not contain herself any longer.. "I read in the book of Genesis in the Bible that an uncle of Noah, Tubal Cain was gifted in working with iron and bronze, just as Noah was gifted from God in building the ark." She saw Philip's eyelids closing and said, "Philip, we must say goodbye to you now and perhaps we will see you in Paris as Fredrico has suggested we join you there. We will be praying for your surgery."

She helped Doug rise from the lounge chair and he went over to the bed to shake Philip's hand as Margaret drew the shade. Signor Ricatto managed to stand up and the three left the room in silence. Signor Ricatto rested his arm on Doug's shoulder and Doug had to say, "Sorry old chap. That's my sore shoulder. I'll come around to the other side". Margaret, who had been trailing behind, moved forward to take Signor's elbow, and so the Parkers assisted the tottering old curator into the elevator to find Carlo sitting in the emergency waiting room. "Carlo?" Doug began, "Could we give Signor Ricatto a lift, to wherever he would like to go?"

"Home." wheezed the curator

"Of course," Carlo replied "I've driven Signor Ricatto home many times when he and. Philip were about their business."

Signor Ricatto sat in the front passenger seat while the Parkers relaxed in the back, too tired for conversation. Carlo turned on the air conditioning so the florid complexion of the Signor paled in the comfort. Carlo knew the route to Volterra as the Bentley easily climbed the tortuous limestone hills.

They passed Sunday afternoon in Tuscany, cruising along the heights above the blue coast until Carlo stopped in the old village and discharged their passenger. Margaret felt constrained to assist the lethargic figure up a few steps outside a red brick three storey house. Returning to the car she said, "The poor old fellow. Perhaps he should look for another line of work."

Carlo guffawed. "He'll retire on a hefty pension, and he enjoys the publicity. I guarantee he will be on the evening telecast. We should watch the news ourselves. I'm sure they'll have some footage with Philip, too. I was talking to the film crew in the hospital parking lot. I didn't dare tell them that you were in the vicinity, Signor Parker, or they might have followed us all afternoon. Surely, you've heard of the famous Italian paparazzi. If they knew where you were staying they'd set up camp in the parking lot." Carlo pulled up to a promontory in a park where families were enjoying the sunshine stretched out on blankets on the grass as younger children kicked soccer balls lazily and teen agers played badminton under the trees. Hibachis roasted sausages and boiled tea kettles. Wine bottles flourished among the groups of men squatting on their heels laughing and enjoying the bonhomie. Pointing to a distant island, Carlo said, "That's Elba where Napoleon spent several years in exile. And beyond, that is Corsica, the land of his birth where he entertained the grandiose plan to conquer the world."

The Parkers shielded their eyes against the bright reflection on the sea. "Well, Carlo," Doug said, "Would you like to stretch your legs for awhile? I believe I see a gelato booth over there."

Margaret smiled. "That's a good idea, dear."

He fumbled in his pocket for the lira. "What flavour will you have?" They stood in front of a cabinet of a colourful assortment of ices.

Walking back to the car, Carlo asked, "Is there anything else you would like to see?"

Doug glanced at Margaret who shook her head. "I feel weary," he said. I'd like to go back to the condo and lie down. Fortunately the shoulder isn't giving me any grief but we're on a holiday and I think we could all use some rest."

Carlo said, "That's the best idea. Sophie will have a hot meal waiting for us. She is an excellent cook. Fredrico and Philip are always pleased with her fare."

"Philip told me to thank her muchly for the truffles," Margaret added "And Doug, remember you're to call Michael tonight around eight o'clock."

They passed the rest of the day in the luxury of travel and the comfort of the huge bed above the rolling breakers, and amid the aromas from the four course meal Sophie had prepared for their supper … a green salad followed by a pasta dish with a spicy pesto sauce. When the Parkers thought they could eat no more, Sophie served a tender roasted chicken breast with steamed cauliflower, snow peas and baby carrots. A light dessert course followed, caramel tiramisu, smothered in whipped cream.

As they carried their coffee cups into the lounge, Margaret asked, "Sophie, how do you stay so slim eating like this? I've probably gained five pounds since we arrived. Doug put his arm around her waist and pinched her lightly. "Don't you believe her Sophie. I'm enjoying all of this. Canadian cooking can be kind of dull compared to Italy."

They reached the lounge and settled themselves in front of the television set. "Did you attend cooking school?" Margaret asked

"No," Sophie replied. "I went to secretarial school, but my father was a chef in a large hotel and so I learned from him. When I graduated from school I went to Victory Film Studio to work in the office for Ozzie about the same time Fredrico began his career.. I loved working for Ozzie. He was such a nice man. After Ozzie died, Fredrico asked me if I would continue on looking after his affairs and household here in Tarquinia. Carlo was his chauffeur and we saw a lot of each other, so we married with Fredrico's blessing"

"I've met Tina," Margaret said. "She seems to manage his affairs too. We went to the house at the vineyard."

"Ah, yes," Sophie said. "She is a very clever girl. But her mother manages the house there beautifully. Tina handles much of the scripting and developmental work on the projects. Fredrico is fortunate to have her assistance. A young man who works at the studio is courting her now. And her mother is happy because she stays at home with the family." Sophie sipped her coffee. "Fredrico is a very considerate employer, both here and there. A cleaning service from Siena comes in to do the heavy work and whenever he hosts a function a caterer is hired.. And here, a housemaid comes in to clean up after the evening meal."

Margaret smiled. "I thought I would help you with the dishes while Doug calls his children. Perhaps you could speak to the operator about reversing the charges for him?"

"Certainly not." Sophie replied. "Fredrico told me you would be making these calls and I was to assist you getting the overseas operator."

Margaret nodded. "Fredrico is a very generous man."

Sophie smiled. "He takes great pleasure in helping others and making arrangements. Do you know what he has planned for you for the next few days?"

Margaret shook her head. "Please tell me, Sophie. Tomorrow, we must get in touch with a Dr. Savino at the hospital in Tarquinia."

Sophie smiled. "You have an appointment with him at nine o'clock in the morning and then he has planned that we drive to Florence."

"Florence!" Margaret clapped her cheeks "How far is it to Florence?"

"About a two hour drive, if the traffic is good. I am to accompany you, Fredrico knows how much I love Florence, the shopping and the art and sculptures of the Italian Renaissance. We are to stay overnight at the Convent of the Little Sisters. It is in a charming location outside the city. And then the next day we are to go on to Venice."

"Good heavens! I had no idea when I told him what I wanted to do in Italy!"

Sophie chuckled. "He has also made arrangements for tickets to the opera in Milan the next evening.."

"The opera! Which one?" Margaret turned to Doug who smiled.

"Madam Butterfly." Sophie set her cup and saucer onto the coffee table and turned her head to the sound of the elevator door opening in the foyer "Excuse me, I must go and see Rose. She returned shortly bearing a tray with a coffee pot and a cream pitcher and a sugar bowl. Margaret watched her serve the men and shook her head at their good fortune to fall into the benevolent graces of Fredrico.

When Sophie returned to sit on the sofa, Margaret sipped her coffee and asked "What does one wear to the opera?"

"It's not formal dress," Sophie replied." Men wear a shirt and tie and jacket, and a day dress for us will be suitable. If it were the opening of the season, it would be tuxedos, top hats, evening gowns, furs and even a tiara or two."

Margaret smiled, "I'm really looking forward to these next two days," she said, and then the serious consideration of Doug's situation clouded her conscience and she became silent in prayer, *"Oh God, please God, don't let anything happen to Doug!"*

Chapter Seven

AFTER BREAKFAST ON Monday morning, the Parkers packed their bags and Carlo loaded them with his valise, and Sophie's into the trunk of the Bentley and drove into a large courtyard before a three story brown brick hospital in Tarquinia. Inquiring at the entrance for Dr. Savino, they were directed down a long spacious corridor with patient's rooms to each side. Many of the wards appeared to be uninhabited as white coverlets were neatly spread across narrow beds with white iron bedsteads reminding Margaret of the hospital in Siena. Nervously, she reached for Doug's hand as they came to the office door of Dr. Savino, where a receptionist rose and enquired, "Signor Parker? Please come this way." She led them into an office where a round, bespectacled man with a heavy black beard and short curly black hair sat behind a cluttered desk. He gestured them to a chair and asked, "And you are Signora Parker?" When she smiled, he asked the secretary to bring another chair and sitting on a corner of the desk, he hesitated, "I've seen Dr. Matera's report and the results of your blood test." The Parkers held their collective breaths. He leaned toward Doug and asked, "May I see your hand?" He examined Doug's palm carefully. "That was a nasty gash and occurred when?"

"Over a week ago." He produced his jackknife. "I was using this to tear my shirt into strips to use as a dressing on Mr. Longfellow's leg that was bleeding quite a bit. I suppose I should say profusely."

"And your palm?" Dr. Savino asked, "Did it bleed profusely?"

Doug glanced at Margaret who said, "Yes. I did manage to put a pad on it and wrap it tightly."

Dr. Savino replied, "That is good. So you can say, once the palm was bandaged it never came directly in touch with Signor Longfellow's wound."

The Parkers furrowed their brows to remember. Doug cleared his throat. "I think you can say that is the case. The only blood on my bandage came from my own palm."

"And you?" Dr Savino said, looking at Margaret, "You had no cuts on your hands as you tended to Signor Longfellow?"

She examined her fingers for hangnails. "No," she replied. "I'm clear."

Dr. Savino picked up the papers in front of him. The blood reports from Dr. Matera show that you are free of the H I V virus. There are no antibodies in your system. Nevertheless the interval between the time of your injury and the blood test may be too short for your body to have started defending itself against the virus. Now we will do another test to check. I think I should check your blood too, Signora. Signor Longfellow's blood is very dangerous. We must not take any chances, given his present condition. And how is your shoulder now? Is there much pain?"

"No," Doug replied. "I'm feeling quite well". Dr. Savino examined his arm and collar bone and showed him several exercises he should do on a daily basis to stretch the muscles and strengthen them. At the end of the consultation, Dr Savino said "I think you are an extremely fortunate man considering the height you had fallen and your contact with HI V blood. Now I will draw a blood sample from each of you and have the results ready for you in a week's time."

Expressing their gratitude, the Parkers walked the long corridor to meet Carlo in the courtyard. Sophie raised her eyebrows as they climbed into the car and she poured each of them a cup of tea from a thermos in a picnic basket. "Is everything all right?" she asked. "Fredrico will be calling again. He is anxious to know how you are."

"We had a good report," Doug replied. "Did Fredrico say anything about the conditions of his friends?"

Sophie reported, "Philip arrived safely last evening after a very tiring trip and Jean Paul is now in the operating theater having part of his lung removed." Margaret watched as nurses pushed old wooden wheel chairs out to the courtyard, their occupants wrapped in woolen shawls to pass the time watching the local traffic of housewives pushing grocery carts and mothers pushing prams accompanied by toddlers.

Carlo drove slowly along the narrow streets and stopped at a gasoline station before entering the autostrada. The cell phone buzzed and Carlo gave Fredrico the report that Dr. Savino had given to the Parkers. When Carlo resumed his seat he told his audience that Jean Paul was still in surgery and Philip was to be operated on immediately because the doctors considered the tumour too advanced to be ignored any longer. The Parisian medical team commended Dr. Matera for his quick diagnosis and now they were examining Fredrico for the same condition. The women gazed at each other and clamped their hands to their cheeks simultaneously. "Oh Sophie!" Margaret said, "How can we enjoy ourselves this afternoon when poor Fredrico is going through such a bad time all alone? We must pray for him." She closed her eyes and leaned her head back on the soft cushions of the back seat.

Doug watched and said to Carlo, "Okay Carlo, I'll pray and you drive."

They encountered heavy traffic all the way to Siena. The sun shone brightly on the farmland where ploughs and harrows worked the grey clay soil. Entering the mountainous terrain of the Appennines, they found the traffic had slowed. "It's the weekenders," Carlo said. "There are many chalets and vacation cottages here where the Milanese and Pisans spend their time enjoying the cool fresh air away from the smog of the industrial north. Azalea bushes bloomed on the median and Margaret spied a group of towers on the horizon. Inquiring of Sophie about them, she learned they were about to come to the hill town of San Gimigano. "These towers are Italy's mediaeval sky scrapers," Sophie explained. "The vineyards here produce the Vernaccia di Gimigano. It is delicious, my favourite of all the wines to drink with a fish dinner. And now we are coming to the turnoff for the Chianti wine district."

Margaret smiled, "I'm afraid Sophie, you're talking to the wrong person because I choose not to drink wine."

Sophie frowned. "But why? Have you ever tasted fine wine?"

"Yes," Margaret confessed. "Long ago, I was at a luncheon with my friends at an Italian restaurant. I had a glass of sweet red wine. It went to my head, my neck, and even my arms became numb and I was afraid that I wouldn't be able to return to work for the rest of the day

From the front seat, Doug said, "You never told me that story."

"It's true," she replied. "But since then, I choose not to drink alcohol of any kind and that's the end of my story."

The Bentley purred over the rolling landscape and crested a hill overlooking a green basin where flocks of sheep grazed. In the middle of the basin was the city of Florence with the sparkling Arno River winding through it past the towers and distinctive cupola of the Duomo and the red tiled rooftops. Carlo announced, "We are coming to the city of Florence and I'll stop at the Convent of the Little Sisters to check on our reservations for tonight."

Doug chuckled. "Will the little sisters permit men to sleep in their convent?"

"Of course," Sophie replied. "Fredrico made the reservations himself. He has contributed to the financial needs of the sisters."

"It's an odd name," Margaret mused. "Where did it originate.?"

Sophie cleared her throat. "You have heard of Galileo Galilei?"

"Yes, of course. He invented the telescope, didn't he?"

"More than that," Sophie replied. "Galileo lived in Florence but fell into disfavour with the Vatican because, when he learned of Copernicus who had the audacity to suggest that the earth was not the center of the universe. Galileo wrote many books on the subject. He used his telescope to prove that Copernicus was absolutely correct.. Florence became flooded with mathematicians to listen to Galileo. He had two daughters, Marie Celeste who took holy orders here at this convent, and aided her father greatly in his correspondence.

The younger daughter joined her sister and the two of them lived here venturing out on occasion to care for their aged father and several other victims of the plague that swept through Italy in the fourteenth century. Several wealthy families supported the sisters in their endeavours. The abbesses chose to ignore the protests of the Vatican far away than force the sisters to make a choice between Rome and their adored father."

Carlo stopped the car in front of an office. "I'll pick up the tickets for the Academy and the Uffizi Gallery.." "I'm coming with you," Doug said. "We will pay for our tickets and these accommodations."

"But Fredrico said…." Carlo protested.

"Never mind what Fredrico said." Doug interjected. "I insist on paying our own way."

As the two men left, Margaret smiled as she looked around at the row of small buildings, arranged around a courtyard with pots of azalea bushes beside the doors. Sophie joined her. "Come around the back," she suggested, "I'll show you where Galileo's daughters tended their gardens of herbs that they used to make medicines and potions." The vegetable gardens for the community had been carefully tended with a wire fence around the neat beds. "The sisters have to keep their sheep away from their produce."

"Sheep?" Margaret raised her eyebrows. "They raise sheep?"

"Yes," Sophie replied." This area of Italy produces some of the finest wools on the market. The sisters here, have fleeces, and their woolen products are beautiful. When their craft store opens after a siesta you can see for yourself."

The men had finished their negotiations and were moving the luggage into the small cabin like rooms. "Isn't this nice," Margaret said as she tested the firmness of the mattress and examined the small clean bathroom. I think we should bring in some of those pillows from the car for your shoulder, darling."

Carlo drove toward the city, and on the ring road, he stopped at an intersection to converse with Sophie about a time and a meeting place. They stepped out of the car in front of a large church and crossed a huge piazza, a quiet oasis away from a very busy street.

They then turned onto a narrow side street where a long line of tourists waited to enter the Gallery del Academia. Sophie waved her ticket and before the Parkers realized it, they were standing in a well lighted room with mouths agape in front of a colossal figure, the Michelangelo sculpture of David, the shepherd king of Israel. Margaret turned to Doug who stood transfixed. They drew closer to the barrier surrounding the statue. "Wow! Michelangelo was some sculptor!" he exclaimed. "Look. The streaks in the marble even look like veins in his legs!"

They drew back with Sophie and Carlo to gaze at the statue… Margaret cocked her head to one side. "I'm afraid to be critical but I think his head is too large for his body."

"I agree" Carlo decided. "Definitely too big. "But aren't his arms too large compared to the size of his chest ?… And his hands are too big for his arms."

"I'm ashamed of us," Sophie added. "What do we know? We're too critical."

Margaret replied "Well I know one thing that isn't right." The others turned to her and she stood her ground. "I don't pretend to be an expert on men's genitals but this David, who was Jewish, isn't circumcised, and, he would have been circumcised as a baby. I don't want to stand here criticizing Michelangelo's masterpiece, I just want to enjoy it."

An official came along urging the crowds to hasten because of the crowd waiting outside. Reluctantly they moved out of the building with backward glances. Upon reaching the street Sophie directed their steps down the street toward the huge striped Duomo. Gazing upward, they were unable to see the cupola towering overhead. Traversing the length of the Gothic structure they came to the front of the cathedral, where across the street, stood the squat rounded Baptistery with the famous bronze doors sculpted by Ghiberti of the gates of paradise and the gates of hell. Turning, they entered the long nave of the Duomo through colourful stained glass doors and admired the marble floor extending the length to the altar. Sophie pointed to a bronze bust of Brunelleschi the architect of the Duomo whose tomb lay in the crypt below. They ambled toward the narthex. admiring the frescoes on the walls between the arched windows. Eventually, they came to the altar beneath the dome soaring three hundred feet above.. Doug noticed people on a walkway. "Say! I think I'd like to go up there." When they went outside to find the stairway, enclosed and gloomy, Margaret shrank from entering, remembering her claustrophobia. "I don't want to go in there."

"Neither do I", said Sophie. "Let's sit in the shade, Margaret."

Doug went on into the entrance and returned shortly to join them at the Baptistery and said, "There were too many red-faced tourists huffing and puffing. I don't want to be a cardiac casualty."

"It's quite a sight isn't it," Sophie said. "The Medici family didn't like the way the cathedral had been finished in the stucco, so centuries later, they paid the cost to refinish the outside in this unusual striping. At the same time the campanile, the bell tower was added. The Medici family was extremely powerful in the Vatican, and banking throughout Europe, and often married their daughters to Kings. Later, after a cup of tea, we will visit the Uffizi gallery which was once the office of the banker the grand Duke Cosmo Medici and later was modified to hold the family's art collection of masterpieces."

After viewing a bewildering collection of 'Madonnas and Child' in the three storey gallery, Margaret said, "I feel overwhelmed and that cup of tea sounds like a very good idea."

Doug took her arm. "You do look pale, dear. Are you feeling sick?"

"No," she replied. "I guess I'm tired and have seen too many beautiful things."

Sophie took her other arm and said, "I've heard of this happening to tourists. There's a name for it. It's some kind of syndrome that people get in Florence. The same thing happens to people in Jerusalem. They are overcome physically by the sights of the city. We will cross the street to this piazza and find a quiet table in the shade."

Sipping her tea, Margaret sighed and said, "There. I feel much better. There's nothing left to see in Florence is there?"

Sophie threw back her head and laughed. "Have you ever heard of the bonfire of the vanities?"

Margaret replied, "Maybe?. What is it?"

Sophie leaned forward and asked, "Have you heard of Savonarola?"

"Vaguely," Margaret replied. "Who was he?"

"Savonarola," Sophie began, "was a Dominican monk who preached against the decadence of the Florentine lifestyle. He preached on hell and urged people to destroy their books and art that was pornographic so he started a huge bonfire in the Piazza Santa Croce. The Medici family were convicted that they too, lived a licentious lifestyle, and feared Savonarola's preaching on hell. Through their influence, the Vatican tried Savonarola for sedition against the church. He was found guilty and burned alive on the ashes of his bonfire. Shall we go on and see the tomb of Michelangelo?"

They proceeded on slowly to the Piazza Santa Croce and came to a bronze plaque in the pavement indicating the horrible events of long ago where now, young boys mindlessly kicked soccer balls around the piazza. Before the church of Santa Croce stood several gigantic statues depicting the rape of the Sabine women and a huge statue of Perseus holding aloft the severed head of Medusa with coiling snakes in her hair. Margaret laughed. "Look at this, Doug. Do you remember when I told you about Medusa?"

He grinned, "Yes. I'm looking at her and I'm not turning to stone either."

Sophie was mystified by the exchange but Margaret said, "Oh look! A sculpture of prisoners escaping through the wall? I'm going to have to look up what this means. Do you know it, Sophie?"

Sophie shook her head and replied, "No, but I'll ask Fredrico and we must hurry along to meet Carlo. Just step inside the church and you will see where Michelangelo was buried a hundred years after he died in Rome. which wouldn't release his body for burial in Florence. Galileo's tomb is just across the entrance where he finally received a Christian burial at the behest of the Medici family who decided it was time to rewrite history."

"Would you like to see the Pitti Palace, the home of the Medici family?" Sophie asked.

"Please forgive me, Sophie," Margaret replied. "I can't take in any more works of art. Today has been utterly fantastic beyond my wildest imagination."

"Well," Doug interjected. "Let's go shopping. I want to buy some postcards and get batteries for my camera."

They continued along the river walk behind the Uffizi Gallery and came to the Ponte Vecchio, an old historic bridge spanning the Arno River with shops on either side of the street.. Margaret stopped to buy silver bracelets for her daughters-in law while Sophie expertly haggled with the silversmith and a satisfied Margaret joined her husband selecting postcards for his friends in New Lancaster. They continued on through the busy streets of Florence where a brisk trade in leather goods with outlandish prices shocking the Parkers as they examined coats and jackets. Sophie pointed out the Pitti Palace with its formal gardens on the commercial side of the Arno. She pointed to Carlo sitting at a table under the trees in a café across the street. Leaving behind the rows of antique shops they managed to dodge the kamikazi cars and reached the safety of Carlo's table. Doug said to their guides, "We are in your hands. What should we order?"

Sophie took the menu as Carlo said, "I've been watching people enjoying the lamb chops."

Sophie said, "For the first course, let's have the Milanese linguini, and then, the resotto ragu looks good. It's ground beef with tomatoes and rice and a green salad on the side. The waiter brought a loaf of bread which they dipped in the seasoned olive oil on a plate in the center of the table. While they were drinking their coffee, the pastry chef appeared in his tall frilly white hat and a immaculate white apron covering his round stomach. He visited each table serving chocolate tarts to the patrons. When he came to their table they shook their heads patting their stuffed stomachs. Enjoying the ambience of the restaurant with mandolins playing nearby, they were content to remain in the sunshine, but the waiter hovered anxiously around their table after they had paid the bill. Carlo stood and said, "We should be on our way. The evening crowd will be along soon and this fellow wants us to clear out." Doug pressed a generous supply of lira into the waiter's hand and Sophie and Carlo led them along the river to the parking lot and the Bentley.

"Now we'll do what many tourists miss," Carlo said. "We are going to Michelangelo Piazza for the sunset." The road wound up to a promontory overlooking the city of Florence. They walked around the bricked courtyard where an iris garden was in full bloom, but it was too early in the season for the rose garden. Sophie pointed out several landmarks they had visited that day. The sun sank lower across the western hills casting shadows on the statue, a smaller copy of Michelangelo's David as they sat and watched the Florentines at their favourite outdoor cafes. Behind them, lights came on in the city and Florence became a magical place with twinkling lights and floodlit bell towers and churches. The Duomo dominated the scene and Margaret asked Doug if he had bought a postcard of Florence at sunset. When he replied, "Yes." She asked," Then will you please keep it for our photo album? We could never take a picture of this with our camera."

Carlo cleared his throat and said, "I think it's time for us to move on. We don't want to disturb the sister at their vespers." When they stepped out of the Bentley in front of their cottages, they heard the sisters singing and imagined the chants of long ago when the world was in turmoil as the age of reason had arrived and the Renaissance was changing the culture of Italy, and new worlds had been discovered..

Doug stretched out on top of the bed in the comfort of his pillows. Margaret sat on the doorstep and listened to the music of the night, crickets chirping and sheep bleating nearby. She hesitated to venture near the bed where, still uncertain of their status with HIV, she felt that any intimacy at this time should be avoided. The problem was solved as Doug began to snore lightly, and after the rigours of the day, he fell fast asleep.

They were awakened by a crowing rooster at dawn and after a quick shower, they dressed, aware of the dress code for opera attendance, Doug put on a fresh white shirt and tan slacks with a light tweed jacket and Margaret shook the wrinkles out of a periwinkle shirtwaist dress, slipped on a pair of sandals and draped a cream coloured sweater over her shoulders. Sophie, looking very trim in a burgundy velvet dress suit and Carl with a matching burgundy velvet jacket over grey slacks, announced. "We are to eat in the refectory this morning. Carlo led the way into an ancient timbered room with rows of scrubbed pine tables. A group of older sisters clad in grey gauze sat on a dais at the far end of the room served by a young postulant wearing a navy dress with a full skirt swinging above her black hose and black sensible walking shoes. Her young fresh face looked out at the world from beneath a navy blue head scarf. She carried a tray of dishes filled with melons and berries and served each of them a bowl silently. The grey sisters ate in silence and to one side a group of postulants, identical to the waitress served themselves from a side board. They walked quietly with hands folded and heads bowed, lifting their chairs slowly to not intrude upon the silence The Parkers and the Perinos did not speak to observe the custom of the convent. The waitress appeared again with a bowl of soft boiled eggs and a basket of rolls. She removed the fruit bowls soundlessly but a spoon clattered to the floor. Glancing around, she quickly stooped to retrieve it. None of the other occupants of the room raised an eyebrow. The postulant then glided to their table with an insulated coffee pot and Sophie poured the brew unobtrusively. The eggs cooked to perfection had been laid fresh that morning. Wiping their chins with the linen napkins, they rose quietly and left the refectory.

"Well," Doug said as they entered the car, "I've eaten in livelier joints. That was quite an experience."

"Yes," Margaret said. "The food was excellent. I wonder how they cook their eggs."

"Fredrico told me," Sophie began "He said, at their matins, they pray that everything they do during the day, they do to the Glory of God. That's how they maintain this place."

Margaret smiled, "I think all of us should do the same thing"

From the front seat, Carlo said, "Now this morning, we are going to follow the Arno River course to Pisa. The cathedral is located in the center of town It is not as beautiful as the Duomo in Florence. The Romanesque style is not as attractive as the Gothic to my way of thinking. But, everyone is entitled to their own opinion."

The streets of Pisa were crowded with tourists in cars from France, Switzerland and Austria, and a younger generation on scooters and raucous motorcycles. Shortly, they came to the cathedral with the campanile beside it, white and lacy, looking like a tall wedding cake. Doug's camera began clicking from every angle. Carlo said, "Stand here on this particular spot to get your picture and I will take Margaret over there and you will have a funny picture." When he and Margaret reached a painted circle he positioned her with her arms outstretched and in Doug's view finder it seemed as if she was holding up the tower.

"That's great," Doug exclaimed. "How did you know that?"

"It's a tourist gimmick," he replied. "Tourists have been supporting the tower for years. If you want to climb to the top, you have to buy a ticket at the booth beside the church. No children under eight years are allowed on the tower. Come over here," Carlo said and he posed Doug holding up the tower and set Margaret holding up Doug. Another jolly tourist entered into the fun and suggested he take a picture of Carlo leaning on Margaret.. They spent the rest of the morning taking pictures of Sophie and Carlo. The tourist insisted on taking pictures of the two couples. They invited him to join them for coffee on the piazza's sidewalk café They learned he was a Texan visiting his son and family at an American air base in Ramstein Germany. near Kaiserslautern and he commented that he was enjoying seeing his son and sampling the mellow brews of the Black Forest taverns. His wife came on the scene to announce she had bought the tickets to climb the tower. The last they saw of Tex was through the open arches somewhere about the eighth level.. They wandered through the church viewing the dark panels where paintings of the life of Christ hung in the gloom. "It's too bad Pisa can't afford the electricity to illuminate these paintings," Margaret murmured.

Sophie replied, "They are saving the money to save the tower from collapsing. If the tower falls, the tourist business will surely suffer. Several years ago, they removed over a hundred tons of earth from below one side of the tower to make it even. They have tried support beams but it was obvious the appearance of the tower suffered.."

Carlo uncrossed his legs in exasperation. "Instead of sitting around here all day, let's go on to Milan and pick up our tickets for this evening."

'Sounds like a plan," Doug agreed. "Do we have reservations at a hotel for tonight?"

"No," Sophie said, "but my brother is head chef at one of the hotels and he said he would make inquiries."

"So, Carlo, it's heigh ho heigh ho. It's off to Milan we go," Doug sang.

Sophie stared at him and Margaret explained to the mystified Perinos. "It's a line from a song the seven dwarfs sang when they went to work leaving Snow White behind at home. You must have read the story when you were children, or have you seen the movie Walt Disney made?"

"Ah yes," Carlo said. "How does it go again?"

And singing "heigh ho, heigh ho, it's off to work we go" they drove through mediaeval villages on mountain tops and deep valleys, until they came to the outskirts of Milan with busy rail yards, a huge airport and grand boulevards leading into the affluent shopping center of the city. They arrived at the Piazza del Duomo and were unable to see the magnificent marble spires on the roof which Sophie told them numbered one hundred and thirty- five. Carlo planned to park at the hotel where Sophie's brother, Charles, was employed. "This is the Grand Hotel de Milan sometimes called The Verdi because the composer lived here for twenty-seven years," Sophie announced. "His apartment with his desk is called the Presidential suite. I will slip in now and see if Charles has made the arrangements." She disappeared through the plate glass doors and returned shortly with her brother, a tall thin man with long brown hair tied in a pony tail behind. The broad smile on Sophie's face assured them that the arrangements had been made. Carlo turned and said, "If you want to go in and register, I'll get the valet to help with our luggage after I park the car." The Parkers were introduced to Charles and followed Sophie and him to the desk in the lobby., dignified by its decor of green velvet upholstery and nineteenth century furniture The lobby appeared to be luxurious without being ostentatious. The rooms above were pleasant with chintz slip covers and a comfortable bed and a French door leading to a small balcony with a wonderful view of the Dolomite mountain range far to the east. They could almost count the marble spires on the roof of the Duomo a short distance away.. Charles stepped onto the balcony of the room next door. "It's a fine view, isn't it. The smog is not too bad today. From here you can see La Scala. Sophie tells me you are going to night. After, you must come to the Don Carlos downstairs and I will cook for you." Smiling and nodding, the Parkers retreated into their room and Margaret asked, "How much is all this costing,?" Doug yawned and lay down on the bed. "Sophie says, it is all taken care of by Fredrico." Margaret shook her head and asked, "How will we ever repay him for all he has done for us? I think we should go to Paris immediately to be with him We can always come back to Italy some other time and we could see Venice then. It must be awfully hard on him, knowing he is as sick as Philip and dealing with Jean Paul's troubles at the same time."

Doug frowned slightly, "You're starting to sound like a mother hen, getting broody over her chicks. I can speak to Carlo about it tonight." She kissed his cheek lightly and went into the bathroom to repair her make-up.

Later in the morning their telephone rang, It was Sophie inquiring if they were ready to set out and explore the city center. The first stop was for lunch at Da Giacomo, the favourite restaurant for the fashion and publishing crowd, bankers and businessmen. The menu centered on seafood and as the patrons studied the menu, they were served a warm pizza with seafood on it. The waiter was knowledgeable and efficient, recommending the specialty, a gnocchi, a savoury seafood with a tomato sauce.. The dessert cart offered a tarte tatin, a Sicilian cassata, a concoction of sponge cake, ricotta and candied fruit. A bank of fresh seafood on ice occupied a far wall. A group of men entered the restaurant and were greeted with a hearty applause. "The soccer team," Carlo explained, "Milan claims two of the oldest and most successful teams in Europe. These guys are almost worshiped by their fans. They can do no wrong. Shall we leave now for La Scala?"

The two couples crossed the Piazza del Duomo to enter the metro station and came to the box office for the La Scala. With no problem Carlo secured their tickets for the evening. "Oh good!" Sophie said when she saw the tickets were situated for the front row of the first balcony. "Would you like to take a tour backstage?" Margaret nodded enthusiastically without consulting Doug who shrugged his shoulders wincing slightly. La Scala was only two blocks along the street from the Duomo and very shortly, they arrived at a crowd gathering outside the doors. Fortunately the guided tour was offered in English, The young man endeared himself to his tour group by saying, "La Scala is closer to a cathedral than an auditorium.. Hearing the opera sung in the magical acoustics is an unparalleled experience." He proceeded to explain how the opera house was repaired after being hit by Allied bombs during the war. He led them backstage to show them the huge curtain where they saw the backdrop of Japanese countryside for the performance that evening. Lying in pieces still to be assembled, was a grey wooden shack that was meant to be Madam Butterfly's home on stilts. They walked down a long corridor lined with posters to see photos of the famous Maria Callas in her various roles. They entered a room containing a selection of antique gramaphones and phonographs, and some recordings of Enrico Caruso. A section of the area was closed where dressing rooms were located. They viewed the old instruments. As the time passed, they emerged into the auditorium and were hushed as the conductor rehearsed some of the string section. Tiptoeing as though on hallowed ground they reached the lobby with the scarlet carpet and gilded banisters and railings.

Margaret spoke softly to the Perinos, "I've heard that Leonardo de Vinci's painting of The Last Supper is here in Milan. Could we squeeze in a peek of it?"

"Of course "Sophie replied. "We'll walk to the Duomo through the Galleria Vittorio Emanuele. This building is the heart and soul of Milanese life beside the Duomo and La Scala. Numerous social functions are held here." They continued on through the barrel vaulted tunnel into the apse of the Duomo the second largest church in the world, second only to St. Peter's in Rome. Marveling at the height of three curving arches, Sophie explained that the cathedral has been described as one of the mightiest Gothic buildings that have ever been created. "Now we must go up to the roof," she said.

Margaret asked," Do we have to climb any narrow stairways?"

"No. We'll take the elevator." They left the elevator amid a forest of gleaming marble spires. Below, lay Milan with myriads of lights, near and far to the airport and the roads leading into the city. Lamps in the villages in the Dolomite mountain range winked at them. Nearby was a huge steel tower which Sophie explained had been erected to prove Milan's dominance over the European efforts at engineering trades. They looked at tourists on a viewing platform of the tower three hundred and thirty feet above the park in the center of the city. Descending to the Duomo, they stopped to gaze at a statue of St Bartholomew, martyred for his faith by being flayed alive. When Margaret realized this old saint was holding his skin, draped around his neck, she felt nauseated by the sight. They left the Duomo through the sacristy doors on either side of the altar and came out onto a street where no auto traffic was allowed. Pedestrians were enjoying the fine evening at the outdoor cafes and Sophie said, "I hope we can get tickets to see the painting."

"Do we need tickets?" Doug asked.

"Yes. The money is necessary to pay for the restoration work. The church was bombed and it cost many lira to repair it after the war." They came to a handsome church with a small cupola. To one side a cloister lay in shadows. Carlo stopped at a small office to one side of the entrance and was relieved to find that tickets were available. Sophie volunteered as a translator for the Parkers who followed an older gentleman to an alcove against an outside wall that offered no protection from dampness seeping through the plaster,. He also explained that Leonardo de Vinci had chosen to work with oil pigments which require dry plaster to adhere to. Then he switched on the lights and told the story of some monks, who not realizing the importance of the work, had attempted to improve its peeling condition by applying a coat of whitewash over it. "And unfortunately, attempts to repair the damage had failed badly" The Parkers peered at the painting noticing the calm hand of a small, dark Judas reaching toward the bread while the other disciples looked distraught and Jesus sat serenely in their midst. The guide pointed out the mystical aspect of threes in the number of the windows and the grouping of the figures. He also mentioned a critic's assessment "The work combines dramatic confusion with mathematical order." The Parkers and Perinos left the church wondering why this work of art could wreak such havoc on the public, suspecting de Vinci had painted his picture with so many suspicious hidden meanings open to wide speculation on the relationships of Jesus with the people portrayed. They agreed they saw nothing to cause such consternation. Stopping to buy ice cream, they walked to La Scala licking their cones and finished them as they reached the open doors to watch limousines discharging the elite of Milanese society. Wiping their lips with handkerchiefs and tissues they entered the lobby where many folks like themselves milled about to find the way to their seats through a number of doors to the auditorium main floor. Sophie led them up several flights of stairs to reach the hallway for the first balcony. They passed open doors for the private boxes and circled past a number of wine bars and rest rooms. Checking their stubs, they shortly were seated in the front row of the balcony. Thrilled, Margaret glanced over the huge hall where people sat hunched over their programs and conversed in hushed voices. She studied the program with the list of performers. "Mirella Freni is Butterfly," she said softly. "I wonder who she is or what country she is from. And Gino Quilico is Pinkerton. I guess Quilico must be Italian but I think his name could be Spanish. It would be too much to expect Pavarotti to fill that roll when there's not the big aria for him to sing. I'm sure Quilico will just be fine." When she realized she was mumbling to herself she closed her mouth and watched glamourous couples take their places in boxed seats where lights glowed at the floor level. The scarlet velvet chairs with scarlet damask wall coverings were all that she had expected La Scala would be, with the gilded railings and chair moldings. The orchestra unobtrusively appeared sliding into their places below the stage. The hushed voices grew silent as the conductor stood and raised his baton.

With a soft whirr the scarlet velvet curtain parted as the sweet melody of Pucini's opera floated heavenward and the pastel scenes of a tranquil Japanese village melded into the overture. With tears in her eyes, Margaret reached for Doug's hand and they watched as a large cast of villagers walked on stage milling about humming. Butterfly stood out among them, and after, a while Pinkerton arrived with several friends dressed in the military whites of the U S A Navy. His attraction to Butterfly became obvious. but subdued and conformed to Japanese standards as they shared tender moments.. The performance of the chorus while Butterfly delivered her baby brought total acclaim from the audience. During the intermission, Margaret gushed, "Isn't it absolutely wonderful! The accoustics in here are everything they're cracked up to be."

"Wait until you hear Butterfly singing Un bel di," Sophie advised.

During the aria, Margaret sat transfixed. When word came from Pinkerton, she wept as Butterfly clutched her child. and dressed him in his little sailor suit to look like his father. She sobbed into her hands as Pinkerton carried his son away and Butterfly lay distraught on the veranda of her humble little shack And when Butterfly ran into the house and reappeared brandishing a large knife which she then plunged into her abdomen and the chorus rose in sorrow and the orchestra volume increased as the curtains closed on a dying Butterfly who recovered to acknowledge a thundering ovation. Doug took Margaret's hand as tears streamed from her eyes, "Come on, dear. Let';s go."

She rose slowly, "Wasn't that the most beautiful thing you have ever seen or heard!" He wiped her face with his handkerchief." I'm sorry I'm making a fool of myself,"

Doug smiled, "You're not the only one. Look around." She did and saw several women weeping unabashedly. "They make me feel better, but not much. I still feel drained."

Reaching the street, Sophie took her arm and said, "I wish you drank. Margaret. You need a little joi de vie." She reached into her handbag and took out a silver flask and raised it to her mouth "I always come prepared to the opera. Have you ever seen La Boheme? Puccini knew how to tug at your heart strings and when Mimi lies dying. There isn't a dry eye in the house. Even Carlo was crying with me, isn't that right Carlo?"

Carlo glanced at Doug and said, "Yes, dear. Let's go off to see what Charles is preparing for us tonight."

Margaret sighed, "I think I've lost my appetite."

Sophie squeezed her arm. "No you haven't. Just wait until you taste Charles' soup. My father sent him to Paris to learn how to make soup. My father met my mother in Paris. She was French and very beautiful."

"Just like you, Sophie", Carlo added.

On that pleasant note the Perinos and Parkers returned to the Verdi and walked down the circular staircase to the Don Carlos Café, named for a mercenary general hired by the Milanese to protect their city from the Venetian doges The legendary soldier, Don Carlos, knew all of his captains by name and the names of their horses, too. Successful in the military campaigns, he ensured Milan became the strongest and foremost city state in all of Italy. "The Don Carlos is one of the few restaurants to remain open after La Scala lets out, and tables are at a premium. The influence of La Scala is evident with sketches of the theater and posters on every wall. The music in the background reflects the current opera."

The Parkers and Perinos supped on a delicious soup with zucchini flowers floating and enriched by porcini mushrooms while a recording of the chorus of Madam Butterfly hummed over head. During supper,

Doug suggested they skip the tour of Venice but go directly to be with Fredrico in his difficulties. The Perinos immediately agreed that they should leave in the morning for France. Touring the lake district as well would bring them around to the Swiss border. Charles took a break from his kitchen duties and joined them at the table pleased that they were enjoying the soup and told them that the favourite dish of the theater patrons was broiled fish on a bed of crisp leeks. The Parkers pleaded that they were still full from dinner and would have a plate of green salad accompanied by a small loaf of fresh bread.. After a wonderful evening, Margaret and Doug said goodnight and went to their room.

As Doug closed the door to the balcony he turned and said, "I wonder where we'll be sleeping tomorrow night? Last night, a convent, and before that Fredrico's on the seacoast and before that, the hospital in Siena. Margaret, I think we're having quite an adventure. She pulled on her nightie and said, "Adventure, yes, but a wonderful time. How does the song go?" and she sang with a little dance. "How are you going to keep them down on the farm after they've seen Pareee?"

Doug laughed "We'll find out tomorrow after we've seen Paree."

Driving from Milan to Lake Garda, they left the autostrada behind, to enjoy the tranquility of the Italian Alps and came to the lovely old mediaeval town of Bergamo. From behind a battered Venetian wall, the town majestically surveyed the countryside. The natural beauty was a relief from the massive cathedrals and handiwork of men. Carlo, an expert driver, negotiated the twisting roads and hairpin turns down to the lakeshore where ferries were unloading cars and passengers on their way to work. Even a group of children filed past to a waiting school bus. Across the lake, the snow capped Swiss Alps rose into the clear blue sky. They watched a funicular railway carrying skiers to the snow fields above. Then, Carlo drove on to the shoreline of Lake Como and continued on to a hotel on Lake Maggiore for breakfast which they enjoyed sitting on a veranda, sheltered from the stiff breeze blowing down the lake. Sophie spoke to a waiter, and before they left, she was soon in possession of a large picnic hamper which Carlo carried out to the trunk of the car.

Relieved that Carlo was at the wheel into Switzerland, Doug watched him navigate the highway bordering steep inclines and precipices by mountain lakes. They came to a hill town, and Carlo parked on a narrow side street where he and Sophie opened the car doors, suggesting the Parkers may enjoy a visit to a clock factory. Before they entered the showroom, Margaret and Doug agreed that they would definitely not purchase another clock since they already had a grandfather clock in their front hall and electric clocks in every room at home. However, they so enjoyed the ambience of the ticking and chiming and cheery cuckoos, and the salesman was so pleasant that they stopped to look at an Alpine chalet where an old man and woman came out on the hour to sit in rocking chairs on their front porch while a small yellow bird appeared, to cheep the hour over their heads, and on the quarter hour, two little cuckoos came out to cheep in unison. The Parkers sighed and smiled at each other, and Sophie came to their side to negotiate the price with the additional costs of shipping the clock to Canada. All of them ambled around the corner to where the car was parked in front of a chocolate shop. The Parkers' waistlines reminded then that they must not indulge after enjoying the Italian cuisine for three weeks. With a few samples in a sac, they climbed into the car to head for the French border on a similar road to the one from Italy.

I wish to dedicate this book to my two sons-in-law, Anil Dhir and Christopher Vinskas who became Mr. Moms for many a time while their wives were absent, taking care of their mother-in-law.

April In Paris

I never knew the charm of spring,
I never met it face to face.
I never knew my heart could sing,
Never missed a warm embrace.
Lyrics to April in Paris E Y Harburg, 1932

April In Paris

Chapter One

CRESTING THE LAST of the Alps they looked out onto a broad green prairie in France and coasted over the foothills. Noticing the tidy hedgerows and swept cobblestone streets, Sophie pointed out they were still in Switzerland. When they came to an isolated farm with a large manure pile outside the barn door next to the house, she said "Now, we are in France." as they noticed the poor fencing around corrals of gaunt horses, ragged ponies and scrawny, dairy cows.

Carlo turned on to a side road and drove through a huge forest. "This is Rambouillet, a magnificent chateau where Napoleon lived for a time. His bathroom is a showplace but we won't take the time to go in and see it. The brick tower over here on the right was built for Francis the first, the earliest recorded of the French Kings. It is said that he and Henry VIIIth of England shared a mistress for a while. She was a sister to Anne Boleyn. Francis loved the arts and brought Leonardo de Vinci to France from Florence. He gave him a house and a pension and Leonardo happily lived out his days in France studying the human body and inventing flying machines and other novelties although his left arm was paralyzed. His friendship with the king of France was so close that he died in Francis' arms. France received the gift of the Mona Lisa which still hangs in the Louvre today".

They skirted the building and discovered the chateau fronted on to a small, dark lake, ringed by a thick pine forest with an island set close to the far shore. "I am told," Sophie said," that there is a dairy on the island built for Marie Antoinette who fancied the simple life as a milk maid when she and Louis XVl came to Rambouillet to escape the summer heat and hectic life of Paris. Louis even imported a flock of merino sheep from Spain, whose descendants still roam the woodlands with hikers and backpackers from Europe who make Rambouillet their destination."

Carlo said, "I'm sorry we don't have time to stay and see the marble hall, but we must press on to Paris." They turned north and shortly noticed signs advertising a picnic area. Turning into the park they stopped at a table and Carlo brought out the picnic hamper. As the gentle wind soughed through the pines they feasted on bread and cheese and hot canapes with a bottle of wine and a thermos of tea. "Ahh," Doug said, "a lunch fit for a king."

Carlo smiled,.. "Actually it is. This is Breteuil, the home of French royalty, famous for its tapestries and a small mahogany table encrusted with pearls and a fortune in precious gems. It also has a museum with dozens of life size figures and a children's park with figures of the characters from story books. Of course, it can't compete with the American Disney Park north of Paris."

"Is all of France so beautiful?" Margaret asked. "I never realized it was so scenic."

Sophie replied, "You will when you look at the art of the French impressionists They painted what they saw outside their windows. Each district has its own charms. What you are seeing today is called The' Ile de France', the province that includes Paris where artists painted the silver poplars and the golden haze in the air above church steeples and roof tops. Many years ago, Paris became too crowded, too sordid, and the bourgeois decided to move out to the rural villages, into the land where Julius Caesar had fought the Gallic tribes in the forests. He was forced to return to Rome, crossing the Rubicon, to preserve his position as leader and ruler of the Roman people and later, Charlemagne established his government in Paris, but afterwards, LouisXlV moved the court to Versailles. Then the population of Paris diminished and even today it is one of the smallest world capitals if you exclude this arca known as L' ile de France."

"Louis XlV, also known as the Sun King, hated Paris because once, when he was a child, his mother Anne of Austria tried to take him to her home. They were captured along the way before they got out of France and the French nobles were rude and rough incurring the child's hatred, so LouisX1V had no misgivings about offending the aristocrats to move to Versailles."

Carlo picked up the lunch basket and said, "Sophie, my dear, we don't have time for a history lesson"

Another chateau came into view, "Maintenon," Sophie said, "the home of the second wife of Louis XlV. It was a morgantic marriage."

"What does that mean?" Margaret asked

"It means," Sophie began, "none of her children could claim a royal title nor she neither. Just because the king found her attractive, though she was socially inferior, she could never be called queen or Lady or anything else."

"That doesn't seem fair," Margaret protested. "Why would she even agree to marry him?"

"For the simplest of reasons," Sophie replied. "Money."

Margaret looked out the window as they crossed a canal leading from the Eur River nearby. Circling around the chateau they were confronted by a huge moss covered three tier aqueduct, which Sophie explained had been built by Louis XlV to provide water to the gardens at Versailles. It had been a huge headache to engineer the project, and, so many workers died in accidents that the entire project was abandoned."

Pressing on, Carlo pointed to a huge steeple ahead, "Chartres cathedral," he said, turning onto a narrow cobblestone street and parking in the center of the picturesque village of old stone houses. "Oh look!" Margaret exclaimed "There's the tour bus from Toronto. Can we stop for a few minutes? I want Doug to meet some old friends of mine."

She spied Bridget and Jim Pearson at the entrance to the cathedral. Taking Doug's hand she hurried across the street to greet the Pearsons and after introductions were made, Jim Pearson said "I understand you are the fellow who discovered the Etruscan tomb

You've become quite a celebrity, man. We've picked up the American publications with the significance of your find. When you get home you'll probably be besieged by the Canadian reporters.. When are you planning to fly home?"

"We're not sure," Doug replied "Our plans are indefinite right now."

Margaret took Bridget aside. "How are your wrists?"

Bridget held out her arms. "We stopped at a hospital in Milan and they had the fibreplast material available. It makes such a difference. Helen has been such a dear. We've become good friends and we just spent a fortune shopping for old books and art prints."

Jim Pearson said, "I must confess, Doug This place is a gold mine if you like old books."

Doug shook his head "I wouldn't even try, Jim. I've got a clutter at home to sort through when we get back." He began edging away toward the Bentley.

"Oh, Margaret," Bridget gushed. "You can't leave now without going inside to see the tunic that belonged to the virgin Mary!"

Margaret opened her eyes wide. "How can you be sure it actually belonged to her?"

Bridget stood her ground." It had to belong to her because it miraculously survived a fire several years ago. Everything else was ruined. This church is so old, it even has an ancient Druid cemetery in the crypt below. We don't have any old places like this in Canada, do we.".

Doug came over and took Margaret's arm to lead her away. "Say goodbye, Margaret. We can't keep the Perinos waiting."

Sophie asked "Did you really meet your friends in Siena? Isn't it a small world. Carlo, Shall we go to the house to see Fredrico?"

"Yes, He' s waiting at the house to hear from the doctors."

The skyline of Paris loomed ahead and Carlo turned on to La rue Chaligny and through a small village of Chesnay where the chestnut trees, heavy with blossoms, drooped over the road. On the right they saw a domed colonnaded chapel which Sophie explained was once part of a convent LouisXV built for his Polish Queen in 1767. On streets leading to their left they could see large hotels. The Bentley slowed to turn onto a drive leading to a modest chateau among the trees and the car stopped beside a stone two storey building covered with vine "Here we are," Sophie said as she opened the car door. "This is the gate house where Jean Paul lives and the chateau is over there," she said, pointing through the trees "It is or was the home of Armand Hammer."

Gathering the luggage, they climbed several steps to the back door inside a glass paned porch They entered a tiled hall which led into a large rustic kitchen with a bowl of purple and yellow pansies on a bare pine table in the center of the room. Open shelves held blue and white crockery,. A brick wall contained a small fire place with embers glowing on the hearth. Fredrico rose from a rocking chair and smiled broadly to welcome them. "So you have arrived in time! Philip and I were hoping you were not delayed by the tourist influx into spring time in France when it is at its loveliest" Margaret kissed his cheek and thought he looked worn and tired "Hubert is upstairs at the moment and will be down shortly for the luggage. I think a cup of tea is in order."

He turned to the hearth and carried a steaming tea kettle. to a big blue teapot. He set the blue and white tea cups on the table. Sophie stooped to get the milk pitcher from the small refrigerator, as Hubert a little man with black hair pasted to his scalp entered the kitchen to set some tea plates on the table with a sugar bowl and cutlery, a plate of butter and a tray of scones. Carlo and Doug carried wooden chairs to the table. Enjoying the repast, they turned the conversation to the medical conditions of Philip and Jean Paul.

"I'm afraid it doesn't sound too good for either of them," Fredrico began as Hubert took out a large handkerchief and blew his nose. Sophie wiped her eyes when she heard that Philip's leg was not healing and had the incision in his groin was not healing as well as the doctors had hoped. "Jean Paul is surviving on a ventilator to help with his breathing. I'm afraid he will have to remain connected to the machine for a long time."

Hubert sniffed and burst into tears. "He has been such a good master to me. I don't know what I will do if he dies."

Fredrico patted his shoulder. "I don't know what any of us will do. At least we have each other. My surgery is set for tomorrow morning. And I intend to survive. Now that you are here, I know I will make a quick recovery." He smiled at the Perinos and Parkers, grouped around the table.

Afterward, Margaret and Doug found themselves consigned to a room with a double bed in a small bedroom with a sloping ceiling under the eaves, Margaret said, "I find it hard to believe that we've ended up in a situation like this. Most tourists, I think, come to Europe and see the sights but we've got caught up with a group of extraordinary people whose lives are far different than any we've known. For instance, a film director and a world famous artist and an archaeologist who has led us into a difficult situation. We won't be going back to Tarquinia now with Fredrico having surgery, so we won't be seeing Dr. Savino to find out the results of our blood tests. Perhaps we should try to see one of the specialists at St. Antoine's tomorrow when we go to the hospital with Fredrico."

The aroma of brewing coffee awakened them in the morning and they rose and dressed to meet Fredrico and Carlo and Sophie assembling in the kitchen with Hubert making an omelet and toast for their breakfast. Fredrico said, "Excuse me but I can't bear to remain in this room with that heavenly aroma. I'm going outside for a walk."

Hubert apologized, "I should have realized that you wouldn't be eating anything this morning because of your surgery." Feeling guilty, the Parkers and Perinos devoured the feast set before them and went outdoors to find Fredrico.

They met him climbing the flagged path that connected the house to the chateau. With the dew on the rose bushes and lilies, the gardens were more beautiful than Margaret had seen in her own back yard. "There's something in the air in France," she said to Doug as they ambled along the path toward Fredrico, who overheard her remark and replied, "Look around you, Margaret. It's April in Paris as the song goes. The chestnut trees are in blossom and the lilacs are so fragrant.".

Carlo drove the Bentley out to the drive as Hubert appeared carrying a small suitcase for Fredrico. He shook his hand and said "Au revoir, monsieur." Fredrico motioned to Doug and Margaret to get into the car.

Sophie smiled and said goodbye to everyone, explaining she would drive into the hospital with Hubert after they had finished with the breakfast dishes. With Fredrico in the front passenger seat, Doug and Margaret watched as they passed the outer fringe of the great park of Versailles and turned onto Rue Ste. Antoine With Fredrico directing, Carlo circled a busy car park and came to the admission office. of Medecine Saint Antoine. The Parkers joined Fredrico inside and waited for Carlo. With the formalities completed they took an elevator to the eighth floor where a nurse showed them into a room which could have been in a luxury hotel. The furnishings had been chosen by a skilled decorator whose intention had clearly been designed to give the patient the sensation of complete luxury. The draperies on the huge window overlooking a green park, were of turquoise velvet and satin, complimented by toss cushions on the single bed with a creamy bedspread and a very thick mattress. A vase with a bouquet of long stem yellow roses rested on a small table.. The art prints on the creamy walls added much to the charm of the room. Fredrico entered the room from the adjoining bath and in his paisley silk bathrobe and blue striped pajamas. He sat down on a wing back chair and crossed his legs. "There's no point in getting into bed until I have to," he said "Would you like to come along and see Philip? Jean Paul isn't well enough for all of us to visit. We will wait for Sophie and Hubert to see Jean Paul. I know it would be hard for him to meet you, Doug and Margaret, because he can't talk right now. Maybe, later on you can say' hello'. Now, Carlo told me that you two had a good report from Dr. Savino, but he wanted to do another blood test on you, just in case. Whatever that means. I think we will call him in Tarquinia to find out the results and if there should be a problem, we will deal with it here. Is that agreeable to you?"

They both nodded their heads eagerly and then Fredrico asked "How did you enjoy Florence and La Scala?"

"It was delightful, Margaret replied. "I have never imagined there could be so much beauty in one city. And Madame Butterfly was wonderful. We loved it and we can never thank you enough, Fredrico."

"Yes" Doug interjected. "We are grateful because we would never have begun to see what we saw without the services of Carlo and Sophie. They are very agreeable travelling companions and we cherish their friendship and yours too. We have been praying for you, Fredrico that God will undertake for you and assist the surgeon who is going to work on you this morning."

"Thank you, Douglas,"

Aa tap was heard on the door and a tall thin doctor entered the room. Fredrico stood and crossed the room to shake his hand and introduce him to Margaret, Douglas and Carlo. Dr, Mallett nodded to each of them and asked Doug if he was the fellow who had come to Philip's rescue. "Fredrico has told me about you and your mishap. I am glad that you have recovered so quickly"

Frederico said, "The Parkers have seen Dr. Savino in Tarquinia. We are waiting to hear the results of their blood test after being exposed to Philip's wounds." Dr. Mallett raised his eyebrows. "But of course. It is important to speak to Dr. Savino immediately. I will have my assistant do that today." He turned to Fredrico, "Are you ready now to see me in the little room down the hall?"

"Yes, I am ready when they decide to come for me. I thought we would go along and visit Philip."

"Ah, yes," Dr. Mallett said, "I've just given him a sedative for the pain. It may be wise to see him now for only a moment."

With Fredrico leading the way, they walked several paces along the corridor and entered a room that was identical to the one they had just left. A hospital bed had replaced the luxurious couch and here, they came to Philip with his leg still strung up on a frame. He was very lethargic, gazed at them with dulled eyes and gave them a wan smile. Fredrico bent down and kissed him tenderly and held his hand. Margaret and Doug were appalled at the change in him since they had last seen him in Siena. A nurse stood at the head of the bed and changed the cold compress on his fevered brow. An intravenous dripped fluids into his left arm. He closed his eyes as Fredrico told him he was soon going into surgery and would see him later. Another kiss and embrace, they left Philip behind. Doug shook his head." He doesn't look at all well, does he?... The poor fellow."

Fredrico wiped his face with his hands, "You wait in my room for Sophie and Hubert, and I'll walk down to the nursing station and see if they're ready for me."

Margaret perched on the end of the bed while Carlo and Doug sat in the upholstered chairs and turned on the television set hanging on the wall to watch the newscasts from England and CNN from America. Sophie and Hubert knocked on the door shortly and said they intended to visit Jean Paul and asked if anyone wanted to join them. Carlo stood up and the Parkers declined, remembering Fredrico's advice. Left to themselves, Doug said, "This sure is some swanky hospital. It makes our hospital at home look like a sterile barn.. I wonder what it costs to stay here?"

Margaret smiled, "We can ask Fredrico but you and I don't have to worry because we won't be staying here, will we? We won't, will we, Doug? Just tell me you are going to be all right."

Some time passed before the door opened and a stretcher rolled into the room. An unconscious Fredrico was transferred quickly and efficiently to the bed. A nurse arrived with a cart on silent rollers as the gurney attendants left the room. Carlo and the Parkers moved to the bedside to look down upon Fredrico who seemed restless and was murmuring Italian phrases.. The nurse took charge of Fredrico and attached his arm to several monitors whose screens were in the wall, masquerading as framed pictures. His friends watched as his temperature and pulse were also recorded on a printer on the cart. The nurse opened the small doors on the side of the cart and brought out a basin and a hand towel. Fetching water from the lavatory, she gently bathed Fredrico's face and discreetly examined his groin and washed off some of the orange skin disinfectant. She recorded the amount of urine in the drainage bottle at the side of the bed and checked the intravenous site in his left arm. She adjusted the shade blocking out the afternoon sun.

Sophie returned to the room wringing her hands. Carlo frowned, "What's the matter, dear? What has happened? Is Jean Paul worse?"

She continued to remain agitated. "No. Oh I don't know. Hubert is in a state because when we got to the room, it was full of his rowdy friends and poor Jean Paul was just lying there helpless and unable to tell them to be quiet. What was the name of that awful one, the one with the bushy black pony tail? You would think this hospital would have some control over who comes in to visit the patients."

The nurse, listening to Sophie, intervened, "Of course it's the hospital's responsibility to protect its patients." She picked up a cell phone and spoke quickly to someone in authority. Turning she smiled and said, "The security is on their way. It is they who will enforce the policy of two visitors to a patient."

Margaret and Doug looked at each other and rolled their eyes. "Carlo, I think Margaret and I shall be going. You and Sophie can tell us about Fredrico when you come home."

Carlo and Sophie looked at each other, "But, Douglas, there's no need for you to leave, besides, how will you get back to Jean Paul's house?"

Doug lifted up a foot. "Margaret and I are used to walking. We need the exercise, don't we, dear."

Margaret smiled, "Of course we do. Besides we can walk home across the beautiful park of Versailles. I'm quite sure I know where to find Jean Paul's house. It's right across the street from the palace where there is a flight of stairs up to a balcony with iron railings."

Carlo protested, "But the park is huge with over two hundred and thirty acres of grass and trees."

Doug replied, "Canada is huge too and Margaret and I are used to walking anyway. So...."

The Parkers said their goodbyes to the nurse, Fredrico, and the Perinos who assured them they would be leaving shortly themselves so they would be home before they reached the house. The Parkers walked through the lobby of the hospital where huge sprays of lilacs and forsythia were arranged in oriental vases. Descending the steps to an extremely busy street, they decided to walk to the next intersection where a traffic light added some semblance of order to the traffic congestion. With the palace in view they proceeded along a side street to purchase a Paris Pass from an attendant for fifty francs and entered the park to approach a village with little houses made of daub and wattle with thatched roofs along winding cobblestone streets. A stream ran along the walkway and they came to a very old water wheel, creaking as it turned slowly "Doug!" Margaret exclaimed, "I do believe we've found Hameau! Remember Fredrico telling us about Marie Antoinette wanting to be a shepherdess.. This is it!"

They meandered through the village viewing tiny vegetable gardens prepared for planting, surprising gaggles of geese that waddled away from them. Pigeons, cooing in the lofts behind the houses, fluttered at their approach. "Well, "Doug said "If Marie Antoinette wanted to be a shepherdess she must have been related to Little Bo Peep. Wasn't she the one who lost her sheep? I don't see any sheep around, nary a lamb."

Margaret chuckled, "Leave them alone and they'll come home wagging their tails behind them.. Douglas, my dear. Besides poetry, you have to remember your nursery rhymes."

Leaving the quaint village they came to an imposing creamy marble edifice with palatial columns, and from the sign outside, they knew this was the Trianon a deluxe building, renovated after the Second World War. which had been a palace built for the mistress of LouisXV, Madame Pompadour. A smaller version stood across the street that they realized was the Petite Trianon where Marie Antoinette had acted out her theatrical yearnings.

They strolled under the huge oak trees and came to a crowded plaza before the imposing palace of Versailles with marble columns across the wide front entrance, a kiosk to one side where they learned they could purchase tickets for several tours in French and English. Margaret picked up a schedule for the tours the following day. They walked along the front of the palace admiring a huge statue of the Sun King, Louis XlV and came to the wrought iron railing which had the initials of M.A. worked into the iron design. They descended to the street, and with a lull in the traffic, dashed across to the entrance of Jean Paul's lane. No cars were in the driveway. "I guess we've arrived before Carlo and Sophie." Doug said "I wonder if the door is open to the porch."

"I doubt it. If I had the art collection in this house, I'd have a burglar alarm system for sure. I hear voices coming from the chateau down below. I wonder what that's all about. It wouldn't be tourists would it? Perhaps we should go and see." Margaret stooped to peer through the lower branches of a pine tree. Turning to Doug, "It's not tourists but some kind of a delivery van."

Doug joined her to see a medium size box van, parked at the rear of the chateau. The burgundy paint with gilt trim and a gilded crest glistened in the sunshine. A sliding door slammed shut and a man with a long black pony tail climbed into the cab as the motor started and the truck backed out of the laneway. Doug rubbed his chin. "I wonder what they were delivering to an empty house? Jean Paul is not in shape to be ordering anything."

As they were musing the possibilities, the Bentley pulled in alongside the house and Sophie hurried toward them, "I'm sorry we've kept you waiting. Fredrico was awake and we didn't want to leave him until the nurse came back from her tea break. You must be very fast walkers to have covered the park so quickly."

Margaret shrugged, "We took our time and found the little village of Hameau It is so quaint, no wonder Marie Antoinette loved to spend her time there, By the way, we just saw a delivery truck down at the chateau which we thought strange. Perhaps Hubert knows something about it"

Sophie frowned." I'll ask him when he returns. We can go in now. I see Carlo has opened the front door."

They walked back along the lane and climbed several steps to enter the foyer where the staircase mounted one wall. Glass paned French doors opened into a parlour. Carlo had already turned on the gas fireplace. A van Gogh reproduction of a vase of sunflowers hanging above the mantel was illuminated by pale sunlight drifting through the large window, facing the busy street A number of antique plush chairs were placed about the room in groups of three or four. Sophie wrinkled her nose at a musty odour hanging in the air. "This house needs a good cleaning. I don't know why Hubert doesn't brighten the place up, or Jean Paul for that matter. Of course he has been away at the sanitarium in Switzerland, which is no excuse for Hubert to let the place go. I'll ask Fredrico to see what he can do about it when he gets out of the hospital."

"Now, Sophie," Carlo protested. "You shouldn't interfere with the way Hubert manages the house for Jean Paul. It needs a woman's touch. But that's not likely to happen." Sophie ran her finger along the top edge of a gilt picture frame. "Just look at the dust. It smells in here like mice live in the upholstery."

"Oooh," said Margaret. "I don't want to sit down in here. Let's go into the kitchen and think about supper.". Sophie moved ahead and put the kettle on for tea. She found lamb chops in the freezer and set potatoes in the sink. Margaret rummaged in various drawers to retrieve a potato peeler.

When Hubert arrived home, he found the table set for supper and several pots steaming on the stove. "Hubert", Sophie began, "Were you expecting a delivery of something down at the chateau?"

Puzzled, he turned to her, "No. Why?

Margaret replied, "When Doug and I arrived we heard voices down there so we saw a burgundy box van with gilt trimmings and a crest on the side. We thought something was being loaded or unloaded and then a man with a bushy black pony tail climbed into the cab and someone else drove away. We didn't look for a license tag because it was too far away to see any name on the van."

Hubert frowned, "I'll get the key and go down there right away. Doug? Carlo? Come with me, please. I don't understand what's going on?" Sophie and Margaret followed the men outdoors and watched as Doug pointed to the previouslocation of the parked van. Hubert opened the door at the rear of the building and then hurried up the slope to the house. "We've been robbed!" he gasped as he rushed in to the telephone. When Carlo and Doug arrived, the women learned that a number of valuable ceramic and porcelain stoves had been stolen from the storage room in the chateau. Carlo directed them into the dining room where a ceramic stove stood in the corner. "Here" he said. "They've made off with thirty of these valuable antiques."

Margaret moved closer to examine the intricate painted designs and the gilt tracings. "My!" she murmured," I've heard of these stoves and never realized they were so beautiful. How much would one have to pay for something like this?"

Carlo scanned the ceiling. "I think about ten thousand francs or maybe more."

Hubert joined them to say, "The police are looking into the matter. I gave them your description of the box van, so they said that would help. We might as well eat supper now. Sophie says the lamb chops are done." As Margaret left the dining room she noticed a number of paintings of still life and decided to examine them carefully in the morning when daylight would illuminate them more clearly.

After breakfast the next morning, she ambled into the dining room to see Jean Paul's collection of copies of Cezanne's still life paintings. Noting one labeled The Blue Vase, she admired the luminous texture of the grey-green tablecloth and the vivid colours of the other items on the table with the vase of flowers. She wondered why the artist had chosen to paint half of a brown bottle with the other half on the frame. More pictures caught her eye as Doug called to her to remind her time was passing for their tour of the palace. They bade Carlo and Sophie farewell and said they would probably return early in the afternoon. Their plans changed and they returned unexpectedly because when they had crossed the street to turn up a wide lane behind the palace they came upon a burgundy box van very much like the one they had seen on the previous afternoon at the chateau. Investigating the location, they discovered an open market for tourists and Parisians, full of antiques and paintings and sculptures. Edging their way through the throng of shoppers they found to their delight a ceramic stove almost identical to the one in Jean Paul's dining room. Margaret nudged Doug, "Look over there. at that man with the bushy black ponytail! Do you suppose he's the guy we saw getting in the truck down at the chateau?"

Doug reached for her hand. "Yes. You're right. Let's get out of here and go back to the house and call the police. Slipping through the crowd unobtrusively and reaching the street, Doug broke out into a full dash with Margaret in her heeled walking shoes wobbling behind him. Breathless, they burst into the kitchen where Carlo and Hubert were enjoying their morning coffee as Sophie washed dishes at the sink. Listening to their discovery, Hubert immediately called the local police and turned with a beaming smile to report a squad of detectives was on the way. Doug smiled and said "I wonder if one of them will be like Inspector Clousseau." With the blank stares, he realized he would have to explain the Hollywood version of the Pink Panther.

To his surprise, Inspector Piedmont did resemble Peter Sellers with a trench coat and a shock of black hair and moustache. After introductions and explanations of what or whom the Parkers had seen the previous afternoon and this very morning at the market close-by. He was especially interested in their description of the man with the black bushy ponytail. Sophie dropped a dish in the sink, and as they turned to look at her, she said," I wonder if that is Jacques Brun a friend of Jean Paul. He was at the hospital yesterday with a few of his rowdy friends."

Pierre Piedmont stood up and said, "Well, we will just go and find out.." The Parkers and Perinos hurried to the front windows of the parlour to watch as a police van emptied itself of gendarmes and they marched away toward the rear of the palace.

"Let's go, too," Doug said, "I want to watch this."

Margaret smiled at Sophie and asked, "Do you want to come and see what happens to Jacques Brun?"

"Yes I do. I want to see he gets what's coming to him. He was supposed to be a friend of Jean Paul. Wait a minute and I'll get my hat."

The men had started down the front steps and turned around to wait for the women before crossing the street. A police officer was guarding the van in the parking lane. By the time they reached the antique store which Doug and Margaret had strolled through that morning they saw several men with their hands secured behind their backs with handcuffs. The elderly owner was shouting instructions to a young clerk who stood behind a cash counter scratching his head. Within minutes several gendarmes had arrived to carry the ceramic stove from the display room outside to the burgundy box van which apparently still contained the remaining loot. Hubert spoke to Inspector Piedmont and learned that he should return to the chateau to open the door for the officers to replace the confiscated property. The Perinos decided to join him but the Parkers, consulting the tour timetable, realized if they hurried they might be able to squeeze in the last tour of the morning. Setting off for the Place des Armes, they entered the Parc de Versailles through huge wrought iron gates and came to the scene of woods, lawns and flowerbeds and fountains galore splashing in Neptune's Basin. They came to the kiosk and chose to tour the palace as others were moving off in horse drawn carriages. Their tour guide, a dapper older gentleman, Albertoise, raised his umbrella as a sign to gather around while he gave them a brief history of Versailles in a secluded corner away from the throngs of tourists "What you are about to see occupies the site of a hunting lodge belonging to Louis Xlll.. His son, Louis XlV was invited to a housewarming party, given by his finance minister at a chateau some distance from Paris. When the King saw the luxurious home filled with fine furniture and silk and gold furnishings, he became incensed that one of his ministers had robbed France to feather his own nest, especially, when all the guests received gifts, diamond tiaras for the ladies and well bred horses for the gentlemen. Louis fired the minister on the spot and hired the architect, the gardener and the designer to build a similar home for himself and hence we have the palace of

Versailles. The family living quarters are known as the chateau. Louis XIV of no small ego, fancied himself to be a personification of the Greek god Apollo and gave notice that he was to be addressed as The Sun King. You will notice out in the courtyard, the brass statue of the king on horse, polished to a dazzling finish in the morning sunshine and of course, from this vantage point, you see the glorious gardens of Versailles. Now, as we enter the palace another glorious scene awaits, the Hall of Mirrors. The hall is over one hundred and twenty-five meters long, thirty meters wide and the ceiling is thirty meters high." Margaret gazed at the gleaming wood floor which stretched almost out of sight with soft light drifting through seventeen arched windows and reflecting off an equal number of arched cornices of mirrors with pale blue walls with the effect of a quiet gentleness. Huge golden candelabra stood along each side of the hall while overhead, crystal chandeliers hung from the arched ceiling painted with pictures of the Greek gods and goddesses outlined by golden beams A red velvet rope prevented admirers from coming too close to the fixtures. A soft "Wow!" escaped Doug's lips. And Margaret smiled "I wouldn't have missed this for all the tea in China." Doug added "All the wine in France." Albertoise turned around to walk backwards to address his group. "The Hall of mirrors is used for state functions. The Treaty of Versailles was drafted and signed here to bring an end to the First World War "Occasionally a ball is held here. Let us walk this way to the apartment de le roi. And you will notice this terrace leads to the smaller apartment de la reine. Many of the furnishings have been removed but you can see the beautiful ceilings and windows that greeted the queen when she opened her eyes to a new day. The toilette has a modestly small porcelain tub with gold and silver fixtures, where' it is reported the queen stood naked, shivering, while two duchesses squabbled over their rightful position to dress the queen in a robe. It is no wonder the Austrian Marie Antoinette hated the French court with all the intrigues and protocol The second and third floors contain the apartments of the nursery and the princes of the blood. Directly above the apartment de le roi are the living quarters of the dauphin, the royal heir, the crown prince. Louis XlV escaped reality where he became the Sun King losing his identity in the Grecian myth of power,. He dedicated himself to assuming the roll of Apollo, the god of fine art and beauty. The apartment consists of seven rooms named for the celestial bodies, known at that time, the planets all revolving around his bright and shining sphere, the sun. First of all we will enter the room of Venus, the goddess of love. You will notice the blue silk wall covering and the huge golden candelabra. Although the furniture has gone, the paintings on the ceiling depict the purpose of the room. The tourists tilted their heads to see scenes of couples lying on couches about the feasting table." This is where Louis entertained his guests with food and wine in abundance and our next room was dedicated to Diana, the goddess of the hunt.". Under a spectacularly painted ceiling the tourists gazed at mounted heads of wild animals, deer, elk,.. And surprisingly, several antique billiard tables were scattered about the room where guests could amuse themselves." The next room with scarlet walls bearing weapons was dedicated to Mars, the god of war." The golden parquet floor shimmered under crystal chandeliers, and gold beams framed the artwork on the ceiling. They continued to another room dedicated to Jupiter the god of law and order. A thick Persian rug covered a dais in the center of the room. Albertoise informed them a throne of solid silver had occupied this place until it was melted down to swell the national treasury after the revolution. Louis used this room as the throne room even though his massive draped bed occupied one corner. Margaret and Doug ambled to another skillfully paneled room dedicated to Apollo. A grand piano occupied one corner near an antique spinet, harpsichord and harps and other stringed instruments on stands were placed near the long windows overlooking the terrace. "Composers of the era often entertained the court in this room." Albertoise directed them to the seventh room, Saturn, the god of harvest and agriculture with rich tapestries and statuary, and next onto the small room of Mercury, the god of commerce and trade.. The finest craftmanship was evident in the writing desks lining the walls. And scattered about the center of the room were card tables and inlaid chequer board tables where

Albertoise was quick to inform them with a sardonic smile the king was an excellent chess player and excelled at cards.

Louis XV held a costume ball here at the festive season. He wanted to celebrate the yew tree so he dressed as a tree and was enchanted by a woman who came as Diana, goddess of the hunt. Louis chased her through the dancers until he caught the elusive quarry. Her name was Jeanne Antoinette, a duchess. She became his mistress, Madame Pompadour, to the distress of his Polish queen. He built a palace for Madame Pompadour. The Grand Trianon which today has been converted into a luxury hotel for guests of the state here in the Park. He also built another palace The Petite Trianon which remains today as a small museum of the possessions of Marie Antoinette, queen of Louis XVl who fled the court etiquette of Versailles. These palaces, lavish for their sole occupants infuriated Parisians who were starving in the streets and when Madame Pompadour went into Paris to shop, the citizens threw mud at her carriage and her person. Even then the royals didn't understand that their outrageous lifestyles fostered hatred until it was too late. The story is told that Marie Antoinette moved to the Petite Trianon and escaped the stench of the chamber pots of the palace. Now without the restraint of the court, Marie Antoinette staged theater productions with she herself taking the starring roles of these little plays written by those playwrights incurring her favour. She performed for her family in the afternoon and they were delighted to see the queen, mother and wife as a maid in a frilly uniform in a silly farce. She proved her vapidity when a servant reported to her, "Madame, the people are hungry, they have no bread" whereupon the Queen, aghast, replied "No bread! Why don't they eat cake?"

"Louis XV decided to drain the swamp around the hunting camp and spent a great deal of money to dig canals and ponds bringing water from the nearby river, the Seine. The water invited the construction of elaborate statuary for the fountains of Versailles.". Albertoise waved his umbrella and announced, "Now we will procede through the gardens to Hameau and the Grand Trianon. If any of you do not wish to walk the distance of two kilometers, you may return to the front entrance of the palace and take a horse drawn carriage to the Petite Trianon where a tour guide will meet you there to show you the treasures of Marie Antoinette in the little museum. Much of the exhibit has been moved to the state Museum in Paris. I will wait for you at the Grand Trianon across the street from the little museum."

Doug turned to Margaret. "Shall we walk or ride?"

"Oh. Let's walk. I wouldn't miss seeing the gardens." They set off beside the huge artificial lake known as Neptune's Basin where a steady spray of water emitted from a triton beside an equally huge seashell. The morning sunshine illumined a large bed of yellow tulips. The walkway wound through beds of crimson tulips and green banks on streams where white snowdrops and purple crocus blanketed the ground.. Hand in hand, they meandered below white drifts of cherry blossoms and entered another grove of pink cherry blossoms where green lawns stretched forth amid towering oaks and chestnut trees bursting into white flowers above, contrasting to the purple clusters on beech trees. They found a wooden arched bridge over a busy canal full of rowboats, to a carpet of daffodils and narcissi. Gardeners working on additional flowerbeds were setting out potted geraniums and a host of other annuals which Margaret could not recognize.. They followed the canal to the cross street which led towards the Trianons where several members of their tour were alighting from the carriages. Albertoise was no where in sight but Doug whispered to Margaret that he needed to find a toilet quickly and didn't want to wait. "Let's head for St. Antoines' now. We've already seen Hameau.. I don't want to look at anymore of the Bourbon Kings' homes."

Margaret said, "I don't mind, and if you've got to go, you've got to go, so let's say goodbye to Albertoise if we can find him. I suppose we should give him a tip."

Doug stared at her and said, "I'll be hanged if I'm going to wait around to give some guy a few francs but I really do have to pee and although it may be the custom in Italy or France, I can't really see myself taking a leak in front of all the tourists in Versailles Besides, what if your friends showed up with their tour bus and saw me going around a corner or behind a tree undoing my zipper." Doug took her hand. "Come on, Margaret. Let's get out of here." They came out of the park just across the street from the front door of the hospital. Deciding not to walk to the corner, he waited for a lull in the morning traffic and dashed across the street with Margaret pelting behind. They came to the front doors of the hospital and found them locked. A security guard questioned them for their reason to visit St Antoine's and explained new security measures were being enforced because of an incident the previous day. While Doug crossed his legs in desperation, Margaret attempted to explain they wanted to visit a friend on the eighth floor who had had surgery and they also had to speak with Dr. Mallett in his office. Following several phone conversations, the security guard permitted them to enter, and much to Doug's relief he found the facilities off the rotunda while Margaret watched the people passing by and enjoyed the beauty of the sprays of fresh cut flowers set on elegant French provincial end tables. He sank into the deep cushions on the sofa beside her with a sigh of relief.. "Shall we find Dr. Mallett first or visit Fredrico?"

She reached for his hand. "I'm afraid to see Dr. Mallett so let's do Fredrico." Doug squeezed her fingers, "Have faith, my love. Everything will be all right. Don't worry about it. We've committed ourselves to the care of God Almighty, so we'll rest in that."

The nursing station on the eighth floor was empty of staff so they proceeded down the hall and were met by Dr. Mallett quietly closing the door of Fredrico's room. He took their arms and said in a subdued voice, "Will you both come with me into my office?" Mystified, the Parkers sat on the proffered wooden chairs in front of the doctor's desk littered with papers. "I'm sorry to tell you Philip Longfellow has just died and I told Frederico. Understandably, he's quite upset and I thought it better to leave him alone for a while. And now that you are here I want to ask you a personal question."

Margaret and Doug leaned forward to listen intently. Dr. Mallett continued "Have you had sexual relations since you were hospitalised, Doug?"

"No. My shoulder was too painful to even consider it. And after I learned about Philip having AI DS from Dr. Matera. I just didn't even think of it because of the possibility of contamination from the cut in my hand. Have you got the report from Dr. Savino in Tarquinia?"

Dr. Mallett flexed his fingers. "Now this adds to the mystery." The Parkers wrinkled their brows. "The blood work taken in Tarquinia indicated that each of you has been infected by the virus. But there are two completely different viruses. The one that your specimen showed, Margaret is a virus usually only seen in Africa and yours, Doug is a mutation of that virus and the one identical to the virus that Philip Long fellow had. Have either of you been in contact with an African who has had AIDS?"

Margaret rubbed her cheeks with trembling hands, and said, "We visited an orphanage in Uganda and I changed a baby's diaper. That's the only thing I can think of. Could that be it?"

Dr. Mallett stood up quickly. "Yes. Exactly. Did you have any cuts on your hands or fingers?"

"Yes," she replied. I had a hangnail that had been bothering me for a few days." She held out her right hand and displayed her little finger which now appeared quite normal. "And I assume that you and your husband have had marital relations since that time.?" Glancing at Doug who smiled, she replied, "Yes, several times. "Oh, Doug! I'm so sorry that I have done this to you. This is all my fault."

"Don't be silly," Doug murmured as he reached across and hugged her.

Dr. Mallett stood up quickly and said," Don't worry about it, Mrs. Parker. You happen to be in the best place in the world, you could possibly be. Here at Ste. Antoines' we have the finest facilities and the best technological advances of anywhere. We will take care of you and we will start right now to test your blood serum for its receptivity to the new drugs which are being developed here in Europe." He spoke through the intercom on his desk and within minutes a nurse entered the room carrying a tray of syringes and test tubes he scribbled some instructions on a requisition while the nurse drew their blood samples. After she had left for the laboratory, Dr. Mallett said, "If you wish to see Fredrico now, he may have composed himself for visitors Will you stop by about this time tomorrow and I will have a report for you then. Please do not be anxious about your situation. I am confident that all will be well because the World Health Organization has been pushing the research on the African strains of the virus because the African pandemic has reached a crisis with the possible loss of an entire generation in some of the countries. There is no fee. The World Health Organization covers the entire cost of the laboratory testing. There is a small charge at our clinic, but Mr. Scalise has insisted that it is included in his and Mr. Longfellow's account. He claims he is responsible for the situation. I suggest you allow him to clear his conscience."

Upon leaving the office, Margaret turned to Doug. "Please hold me, darling. I don't have the strength to handle all of this. I feel overwhelmed like I did when I learned that I had ovarian cancer but I didn't have you then and I didn't have Jesus. But now, I know I can get through this, and I know we can get through it all together. So let's go and see Fredrico. and I wonder how we can comfort him in the loss of his beloved Philip."

They tapped on the door and found Fredrico standing in his robe and gazing out the window. He turned to them slowly to see the compassion in their faces. "You've heard about Philip?" he asked.

"Yes." Doug replied. "Dr. Mallett told us.".

Fredrico stepped toward them and asked eagerly, "Your blood report from Dr. Savino?"

Doug shook his head. "Positive ... both positive."

Fredrico frowned at Margaret, "And you too?"

She reached for his hand. "Doug and I agree that this disease is not going to defeat us in any way because we have God working for us to control it. We have confidence in Dr. Mallett and Jesus to bring us through. Please don't be upset for us. It's important you use all your strength to recover from the operation and remember what I told you about prayer and giving your life to God. How are you feeling, my friend?"

"About as well as can be expected," he replied, "The incision is healing quite well. And Dr Mallett said the biopsy shows that it is the same as Philip had." he passed his hand across his eyes and took a handkerchief from his pocket to blow his nose. "I'm so sorry I infected him with the virus and now, Jean Paul is fighting his own battle. I'm trying to trace this virus and it probably started with Ozzie, and now it has spread to other people I love." He reached out to Doug.. "When you left Canada, you never realized you'd be going home with such a burden."

Doug gazed into his eyes. "Fredrico, don't torment yourself over this. Dr. Mallett has assured us of the best treatment possible, so Margaret and I aren't going to worry about it, are we, dear?"

She smiled bravely. "We are going to trust Jesus to heal us and you, too, Frederico. Now how is Jean Paul today?. I've been admiring his collection of Cezanne's. He has such a gift, doesn't he."

Frederico smiled.. "I just walked to his room to see him. He's doing much better because they've removed his tubes, so he's breathing on his own which is a good sign. He's been moved to the special room where they can monitor him closely and keep out his rowdy friends By the way, I hear that some of them and Jacques Brun robbed the chateau yesterday."

Doug said, "You've heard about that? The chateau seems vulnerable to theft, the way it's hidden in all the trees."

Fredrico eased himself into the wing back chair and stretched his legs clad in blue striped pajamas. "Yes. I just spoke to my lawyer, Claud Brisson. He'll put a security detail on the property. He's my lawyer and takes care of Victory Studio's business in Europe. He came this morning just after Philip had died and he will look after all the arrangements. It was Philip's wish stipulated in his will to be cremated and his ashes to be scattered across the Salisbury Plain near Stonehenge. So I will take care of that after I'm up and about in a few weeks. Perhaps Carlo and Sophie will go with me."

"Could Doug and I be of any help to you, Frederico? It may be quite stressful for you crossing the channel and I think we would be free to travel then ourselves. However long Dr. Mallett's treatments take.."

"Well, thank you. I appreciate your concern. And I'm not sure Carlo and Sophie will be able to travel then because they're due for their spring vacation and I know they want to visit their daughter in Crete.".

Margaret opened her eyes wide. "I didn't know they had a daughter. Sophie never mentioned her. She lives in crete"

Frederco cleared his throat. "I don't want to bear tales, but yes, Sophie had a child long before she came to work for me or met Carlo. Her daughter was taken to Greece as an infant by the father and Sophie has had a difficult time establishing a relationship with her because of the hostility of the Greek women who claimed Angelica as their own with the help of their brother who is the father and lives in Crete, Sophie had a very difficult time getting the international courts to establish her maternal rights of visitation after the kidnapping. I put Claud Brisson to work on her behalf but the wheels of justice grind so slowly."

"Poor Sophie," sighed Margaret. "What a heartache! She never mentioned any of this."

"I know," Fredrico nodded. "She has buried the pain and lives for the spring when she visits Crete."

"Crete?" Doug raised his eyebrows. "I always wanted to visit Crete and see the ruins of the Minoan Empire."

Fredrico smiled. "There's not much to see, Doug, except some paintings on walls and some rough stone work leading to the palace. There's nothing about the minotaur and the labyrinth, but they do have a very fine museum.. You and Margaret could fly to Crete quite easily. Probably, Philip would show you some of the pottery traded to the Etruscans.." Sudden tears filled his eyes. "I'm going to miss Philip terribly. I just can't believe he has gone!"

Margaret and Doug sat quietly watching his struggle. Finally, Margaret rose and walked over to him, laid her hand on his shoulder and said softly. "I know it's hard, Fredrico, but you have the memory of a precious friendship and we'll go now and leave you with those memories." She reached out to Doug who stood and quietly opened the door.

Chapter Two

MARGARET AND DOUG awoke the next morning to the sound of the vacuum cleaner. Doug stirred and rubbed his eyes, "What time is it?" he grumbled.

Margaret squinted at her wrist watch. "Eight, thirty! I wonder what's going on."

"Probably Sophie's cleaning the house for Fredrico's home-coming."

Margaret scrambled out of bed ducking her head to avoid the slanting ceiling. She slipped through the door to the bathroom and dressed quickly. Doug rose and said, "Don't forget we have to go with Hubert when he picks up Fredrico"

"No," she replied. "This is another day of a new adventure. Imagine the two of us being treated for AIDS in a hospital in France! Do you remember what Jack Ferguson said when I told him we wanted to grow old together peacefully."

"Yes," Doug replied. "And he said when we become Christians, we are never granted the option of growing old quietly and peacefully. But thank God, we have the assurance of the Lord always being there no matter where we find ourselves. And here we are today, facing the unknown again."

Margaret kissed his cheek and whispered, "Come on, darling let's go downstairs and face what Sophie and Hubert have planned for this morning."

Descending the stairs, they could see through the glass panes on the French doors that Sophie with a scarf wrapped around her head had turned all of the chairs upside down and was thoroughly rubbing the underside of the padded seats with the nozzle of an antiquated vacuum machine. She raised her head and turned off the motor as she saw the doors open. "I'm so sorry to have wakened you, but I just couldn't let Fredrico come home to this!"

"Think nothing of it," Margaret replied. "We had to get up early anyway to be ready for Dr. Mallett this morning "Where are Hubert and Carlo?"

Sophie readjusted her head scarf. "Hubert's in the kitchen baking croissants. I wanted him to shine these windows but he insisted on having the fresh croissants for Fredrico. I sent Carlo to the market to get some fresh fruit because Fredrico loves fruit salad with the croissants."

Doug glanced around. "Where's the glass cleaner, Sophie? I'm used to polishing stuff."

"And I can help you dust after you've finished in here." Margaret added.

Sophie handed a spray can and cloth to Doug while Margaret went into the kitchen to ask Hubert where to find the dust cloths and furniture polish. He looked up from his mixing bowl and pointed with a floured finger to the pantry across the room. "Thank you for helping us," he said and resumed his dough making. Margaret went into the dining room where Sophie was now attacking the Axminster rug under the table. In order to stay out of her way, Margaret moved on into the parlour where Doug was buffing the glass panels in the French doors, so she decided to polish the wood frames of the upholstered chairs and settee. and the bow window behind the lace curtains. The mantel held few trinkets to delay her progress so she stood on a footstool to dust the frame of the picture of a vase of bright yellow sunflowers. The frame of the Van Gogh copy had been beautifully carved and stained a burnished oak which enhanced the tinted tones of the masterpiece. Back in the dining room she dusted the framed Cezannes and suggested that Doug might "very carefully" polish the glass on the pictures. By the time she and Sophie had finished, Carlo had returned from the market bringing a huge bouquet of yellow roses which Sophie placed in a tall crystal vase on the gleaming walnut table. The aroma of the croissants drew them all to the kitchen for coffee where Hubert had replaced the bowl of tired pansies with a fresh bouquet and Carlo was setting out mugs and plates. With the satisfaction of a completed chore and the joy of anticipating Fredrico's return, they sat in the cheery kitchen and praised Hubert's culinary efforts. Doug glanced at the clock and asked, "Fredrico is being discharged at ten o'clock? And Margaret and I have an appointment then so I suppose we should be on our way." Hubert rose and said, "I'll get the car now."

In a grey misty morning Margaret climbed into the back seat of the Fiat and shivered as Doug and Hubert closed their doors and moved off into the Parisian morning traffic. Reaching the car park of the hospital, Hubert was unable to find a parking space and suggested the Parkers go inside and tell Fredrico that he would be waiting for him outside the admitting entrance. "I'm sure an attendant will accompany him there in a wheel chair, so I'll be watching for him in ten minutes?"

Doug and Margaret agreed and hurried to the eighth floor where they found Fredrico dressed and waiting for them with his bag packed. "I've been along to say goodbye to Jean Paul and he would like to meet you and thank you for your help in saving his treasures. He led them along the corridor and opened the door of a small cubicle where a pale thin man lay in a narrow bed. Margaret extended her hand with a smile. "Hello, Monsieur Claudet. I am a great fan of your art and I'm grateful to have this opportunity to meet you. However, I wish the circumstances were much different." She noticed an oxygen catheter under his nose, with a black ribbon tied over a heavy black mop of hair. "Please don't feel obliged to talk with me," she said. "I always talk too much, so my husband says." She turned to Doug as Fredrico stepped to her side and lay his hand on Jean Paul's shoulder. "These delightful people are the Parkers from Canada. Remember I told you how they saved dear Philip from dying on the hillside at the time of the earthquake?"

Jean Paul closed his eyes, filled with tears and whispered, "Fredrico, what will we do without our Phillip?"

Fredrico shook his head sadly and said, "If I feel well enough in a few days, I plan to take Phillip's ashes home to England. I will come to see you before I leave and I promise to return very soon. You and I have to take a lot of time to recover. So, we should go on a vacation in St. Tropez. You remember that nice house on the quiet beach in the sun. We will get some colour back in our cheeks."

As he bent to kiss Jean Paul's cheek, the door opened and Hubert entered. "I was able to find a parking spot at last," he stated and came alongside the bed. "Do you feel well enough to see inspector Piedmont? He demands that he see you about pressing charges against Jacques Brun because he says that man is the head of a gang of burglars in the east end of the city, and I'm afraid he is insistent on getting a conviction for all of them." Jean Paul closed his eyes and shook his head weakly.

Fredrico leaned down to whisper, "Jean Paul, why don't you see the inspector and get it over with?"

Jean Paul broke out into hoarse sobs. "I can't send Jacques to prison because he is my brother"!

With the ensuing silence, Doug and Margaret looked at each other and moved stealthily toward the door. The nurses' station was opposite and an attractive nurse whom they recognized as Fredrico's former care giver, beckoned to them to join her behind the counter. "Dr. Mallett will see you now. Will you please come with me?" She led them into a small cubicle where two beds were arranged behind a screen. "If you don't mind sharing this room, I'll leave you to change into the gowns laid out for you."

They quickly undressed and climbed into the beds. "This feels odd," said Margaret. I didn't think we would end up in bed this morning. How is your pillow?"

"It's very firm My shoulder doesn't like it." Doug said.

"Mine isn't too bad. Would you like to borrow it?" Margaret asked.

While they were exchanging comforts, the nurse returned with a cart of equipment. "I can find you some more pillows if you would like," she said.. "Soft or firm? I'm here to start your intravenous infusions."

Obediently they held out their left arms and shortly the procedure was accomplished as Dr. Mallett entered the room and sat down at the end of Doug's bed. "Are you ready for your cocktails?"

He held up two bottles of clear fluids. "The laboratory has ascertained which virus is less resistant to each drug." Turning to Margaret he hung a bottle on the pole beside her bed. "You, Margaret, have a virus that is solely of the sub-Saharan strain. And you may have fewer side effects from this infusion than our boy, Douglas here, who now has a mixture of the two viruses, one of which is the usual garden variety, so in essence, you, Douglas are being bombarded by two drugs which will seem toxic after awhile. You may suffer some nausea and diarrhea and lethargy. To put it bluntly you are going to feel like hell.. It's the reaction to the virus that you contracted from Phillip Longfellow, a common virus that is so deadly. We will be treating your friends with this new drug as soon as they can tolerate it after their surgeries. How soon we begin will depend on their blood count of theT4cells. We will check your levels in three days to know how long to continue the infusions. If all goes well we may be able to use some oral doses which will be much easier for you. Of course we are not sure how, much of the drug is neutralized by the stomach acid, so we will monitor your T4 levels very closely.."

The nurse returned with her arms full of pillows which she tucked under Doug's head and he adjusted his shoulder until he was comfortable. Margaret was soon settled and she inquired "Would you tell us your name?"

The nurse straightened the top sheet and smiled, "Je suis Margot Perrier. Voulez vous un cup of tea?"

Doug practised his French, "S' il vous plait, ma'mselle. Pour les deux."

Margaret giggled. "I didn't know you could speak French, dear."

He said, "I read the cereal boxes once in a while, and I pick up a little from the sailors across the lake."

They cranked their beds to a sitting position and were sipping their tea when Fredrico and Hubert arrived to say good-bye. "You look very comfortable," commented Fredrico "Did Dr Mallett say how long this would take?

"Well," Doug replied. "It sounded like I would feel like hell for about three days."

Fredrico frowned and turned to Margaret "I am so sorry for all that has happened to you. 'I can't tell you how grateful I am for all you tried to do for Phillip. But if you are feeling better next week I would like to take you to England with me. You will want to visit Stonehenge and Salisbury Cathedral. And I would like to see Victory in Portsmouth Harbour. Ozzie fell in love with it. It was always his intention to do a documentary on Nelson and the victory at Trafalgar. So now, in his memory I think the studio will go to work on it. I have been in touch with Tina in Siena to get the staff on it soon. Antonio will be arriving in a day or so to set out the plans for the shooting schedule. He will accompany us to England and make the arrangements.. Since Carlo and Sophie will be leaving for Crete shortly, I would appreciate your company."

Doug glanced at Margaret. "Thank you Fredrico for the opportunity to go to Stonehenge. I'm sure we will be well enough to travel by next week, but I'm confused because I understood Dr Mallett wanted to start treating you and Jean Paul with these drugs as soon as you had recovered from your surgery; Will you be able to travel yourself?"

Frederico waved his hand. "Of course I will. I plan to start the treatment today.. Margot, will you summon Dr. Mallett for me now?"

The nurse left the room. Margaret glanced at the bottle hanging over her head. "It's almost empty, Frederico. If you like, I can let you have this bed so you can keep Doug company."

"That's a good idea." he started to release his neck tie when Dr. Mallett entered the room. "Margot tells me you want to start your treatment now, Frederico? I will call the lab and see if they have any serum on hand."

Margaret said, "I'll change into my street clothes and be ready to return home with Hubert. But first Margot will have to disconnect me."

Shortly Dr. Mallett returned with another bottle of serum and Margot efficiently dispatched Margaret with a band-aid on her fore arm and had an intravenous solution running into Fredrico's arm. Hubert took Margaret's elbow and suggested they be on their way to tell the Perrinos of the change in plans. After a quick kiss goodbye, Margaret assured Doug they would be waiting for him and Fredrico that afternoon with the croissants and hot coffee. Hubert guided her into the corridor and the elevator and outside into a grey Parisian morning. The traffic had lessened and they reached home in time. to watch Carlo and Sophie loading their luggage into the Bentley. Disappointed that Fredrico was not with them, they hugged Margaret good-bye and asked her to convey their regrets to Doug and Fredrico. Aware that it was unlikely they would meet again, Margaret kissed them and wished them a happy reunion with their daughter. As the Bentley turned out onto the road leading toward the Italian border, Hubert waved goodbye, turned to Margaret and asked "What shall we do now?" She looked at him blankly until he asked, "Would you like to see the chateau?"

"I'd love to see it. Jean Paul wouldn't mind if I was snooping to see how the rich and famous lived in the nineteen thirties."

"Of course he wouldn't mind," Hubert replied. "I'll just slip inside and get the key."

Margaret listened to the sounds of traffic and stepped in to the grove of pine trees where a soft hush was interrupted by the crows high in the oak trees behind the chateau. She meandered slowly along the flagstone path toward the fieldstone structure until Hubert caught up to her and followed until they reached the courtyard where Jacques Brun had parked the truck. Hubert swung the wide doors open to reveal a dark storage area where many crates containing the stoves were aligned. From there he led her up several steps into a large kitchen with windows overlooking the stream which flowed into the Seine beyond the chateau. The kitchen held a huge black stove with a wicker wood box in the corner. Various pine tables were set about the red brick floor and pine cabinets lined the walls beside a cast iron enamel sink with a n antiquated water pump.. Leading her into a huge dining room with a bow window at one end overlooking an untidy garden where the stream wound its course through banks of daffodils." This was a most beautiful room so I've heard, "Hubert explained. "Jean Paul sent all the candelabra and china to auction after Hammer's death. An antique dealer calls constantly to inquire if he might acquire the furniture, the table and dozen chairs and other furnishings in the chateau. I don't know why Jean Paul won't sell them because the antique dealer has warned him that they might deteriorate because of infestations of woodworm. Perhaps the Jacques Brun. episode will persuade him to part with his antiques, When we first met, Jean Paul was almost a starving artist until Armand Hammer paid him his commission. After he inherited the chateau, he was forced to sell the silver and china because he had almost no money to pay for heating and electricity in the chateau. That was when he decided to move up to the gatehouse." They ambled on into the next room which was a huge foyer with a marble floor and a white marble staircase, curving to the second floor. A wide stained glass window on the wall behind the staircase drew the golden afternoon sunshine into the icy interior. Hubert turned to open a solid wooden door into a glass vestibule at the front of the chateau.

"Oh look! Margaret exclaimed. "A limousine has just pulled into the drive."

"I t must be Fredrico," Hubert said and turned to hurry up the flagstone steps leading to the house.

"And there he is, and Doug too," Margaret cried as she rushed past Hubert on the path. She threw her arms around Doug and drew back quickly when she noticed he was carrying a small plastic basin. "Oh, darling, have you been sick?".

Frederico held out his basin and explained, "We both are, in more ways than one. I'm glad this house has two lavatories." He turned and quickly followed Hubert into the house. Doug took Margaret's hand and rushed upstairs. She sat on the rim of the bathtub and held the plastic basin as he retched, and she wiped his face with a cold damp cloth. Finished, he went over to lie down on the bed and she covered him with an extra blanket and lay beside him "I'm so sorry for you, darling. Can I do anything to help you?"

"Dr. Mallett said I would feel like hell. This isn't like the hell I was in in the tomb but I just feel rotten, like I want to close my eyes and shut out the world."

"Alright, darling, I won't bother you. I'll go downstairs and see what Hubert is doing with Fredrico."

The kitchen was empty when she looked for Hubert and heard the sound of voices and a toilet flushing at the back of the house. She poured a cup of coffee for herself and set out another mug for Hubert who joined her presently. He placed a jar of strawberry jam on the table and buttered the croissants. "Well, Margaret. I think you and I are going to have a few croissants to eat for the next few days if Doug feels anything like Fredrico."

She smiled bleakly. "I don't know Hubert but I had a treatment today but it hasn't affected me yet. Dr. Mallett didn't say what I could expect, so maybe I'll get off lightly, I hope."

"I hope so too," Hubert replied. "This place can be very lonely when I'm here alone and if all of you go to bed, I won't know what to do. If Jean Paul starts the treatment, I hope he will stay at the hospital because, I'm not a good nurse. Poor Fredrico. Every time he retched, I thought I was going to vomit too."

Margaret glanced out the window over the sink. "Hubert, instead of sitting around in the house, I think I will walk down to the chateau and pick a bouquet of daffodils. They are on Jean Paul's property, aren't they?"

"Oh, yes, of course. The property line extends well across the stream. You will not be trespassing." He rose and took a pair of garden snips from a closet by the backdoor.

Margaret spent a delightful afternoon walking along the banks of the dark stream. She sat on a tree stump in a patch of sunshine to view a white swan family with two cygnets paddling behind their watchful parents and three cygnets perched among the feathers of the pen's back A covey of ducks swam by. Above the rush of traffic sounds she recognized the birdcalls of blue jays and cardinals and ravens. Running her fingers through her hair, she breathed a prayer to God for the beauty of the surroundings, the medical care they were receiving and for the interesting journey they had had in Africa and Italy and now they were about to see England which is where she had planned to go so many years ago. She became aware of someone walking toward her. Fearful, she turned slowly to see a young man of medium height and dark curly hair. His eyes crinkled at the corners as he spoke, "Bon journo, Signora Parker?"

Startled, Margaret asked, "Do I know you? I have met so many people lately that I tend to become confused."

He smiled. "No we have not met before. Hubert told me you had come down to pick daffodils. My name is Antonio Merissa. I am an associate of Fredrico and have come to Paris to do business with him."

She smiled and held out her hand. "I remember Fredrico said that you were coming to work on the film of Lord Nelson and the victory over the French at the Battle of Trafalgar."

He cocked his head to one side and asked, "You are interested in French history?"

"No," she replied. "Yes, I am but I find it all terribly confusing. I only glean snippets of information from conversations my husband has with tour guides. My husband is the one who loves history because he teaches history in a secondary school in Ontario, Canada."

"And it was your husband who fell into the tomb in Tuscany? He has become famous because of his adventure."

"Yes I suppose he has, but it could have killed him. Only the grace of God has saved him from a fatal fall. Unfortunately, Philip Longfellow died from his injuries in the earth slide."

Antonio shook his head." Philip Longfellow died because of his choices made many years ago."

Margaret smiled wryly. "When we started out that day, neither of us, Philip Longfellow, my husband nor I had any idea of what the day would bring forth. We had never met Fredrico or even heard of him, but he has become a steadfast friend and offered us so many opportunities to see Italy and France too and now, of all things. he asked us to accompany him to England..."

"Ah, yes, Fredrico did mention taking along two friends when he went to Stonehenge with Philip's ashes."

"The two friends are my husband, Douglas, and me," she said. "We'll try not to bother you in your work."

"My work," he scoffed. "My work is going to be more complicated than I thought."

Margaret glanced at him with questioning eyes. "Is there a problem?

He shifted his feet. "Yes. Tina. Have you met Tina? Fredrico's assistant?"

She nodded. "Once. She's a lovely girl."

He spoke softly. "Yes, she's a lovely girl, but she made a mistake thinking I could get the information, I needed at the Sorbonne here in Paris. Apparently the French scholars don't like to discuss the English victories and they can contribute nothing to the film on Trafalgar. And so it seems that I will have to enlist the help of Professor Ernest Throckmorton at Oxford. Apparently, he is an authority on the Napoleonic campaigns. And then, there is a vice-admiral Billy Bush at the naval museum in Portsmouth. who can fill in the details. If you are not in a hurry to see Stonehenge, I would like to spend some time in London."

"Antonio, there is no doubt that Doug and I would welcome an opportunity to see London, especially the British Museum as far as Doug is concerned. But right now I must get busy making a bouquet of daffodils." She rose and waded into the patch of yellow., taking care not to crush the flowers under foot. "I wonder how these were planted like this."

"Oh, don't you know?" Antonio asked. "Have you seen the picture Jean Paul Claudet painted of Armand Hammer leaning on a hoe down here by the river?"

"No," she replied." I haven't. Is it up at the house?"

"Probably. I'm sure Fredrico knows where it is. Let me hold those while you gather some more."

After picking a huge bouquet, Margaret realized Hammer had planted the bulbs in such profusion that the patch seemed to be undisturbed. "There she said, taking off her gloves, "I have enough to fill the house. I hope Hubert doesn't mind." She and Antonio walked up the path toward the house and met Doug descending the front steps "Oh, darling, I'm glad you are feeling better. This gentleman is Signor Merissa, Fredrico's man in charge of the Trafalgar film."

"Antonio Merissa," the young man smiled, extending his hand, "And, you are Monsieur Parker?" He turned to return into the house where Hubert waited at the door

"Douglas, just call me, Doug. I'm sorry you have caught Fredrico and myself at a bad time. We spent the morning undergoing treatment at Ste. Antoine's, and I'm afraid we're both a bit off colour. Have you seen Fredrico, yet?

Hubert stepped forward. "Fredrico has finally drifted off to sleep. Let's go into the parlour and I'll bring some coffee."

Doug held up his hand. "None for me, thanks, Hubert. I plan to give my gastric juices a rest today." He wrapped his robe around himself tightly and sank into the nearest soft chair. Margaret perched on the armrest and stroked his forehead. She then followed Hubert into the kitchen to find a vase or two to accommodate the daffodils. Fredrico wandered into the kitchen, yawning and tying the belt on his robe. "I see you have discovered Armand Hammer's garden of daffodils. Come into my bedroom and I'll show you a picture of when they were first planted." He thrust back the heavy drapes covering the window and turned on a lamp to illuminate a small scene of a weary labourer leaning on a hoe beside a tree, regarding a patch of cultivated earth." That man is Armand Hammer, and Jean Paul returned several years later to paint this scene of the finished product.

Margaret gasped slightly at the accompanying picture. "The yellows are so beautiful," she murmured.

"Yes," Fredrico replied. "Jean Paul was very fond of the way van Gogh used the yellows. Have you seen the wheat field he painted outside Arles in southern France?"

"Yes. I did go to an exhibition of Van Gogh in Toronto. That was a long time ago but I still remember it vividly. There was such energy in the painting. You could almost hear the wind rushing across the stocks of grain."

Fredrico smiled at Margaret. "So what do you feel when you look at the daffodils?"

She stepped back to look at the patch of clear yellow in the rays of sunlight streaming down through the trees, and turned to Fredrico. "I feel peace and quietness, near to the heart of God.. Those words come from an old hymn we used to sing. There is a place of quiet rest near to the heart of God."

Frederico turned his head as she sang the lines. "That's beautiful, Margaret. Do you know the rest of it?"

She shook her head. "I'm sorry I don't, but Doug may. He's the singer in the family."

Hubert pushed his head into the room. "Do you two want some coffee?"

Fredrico shook his head. "I'm not eating or drinking anything that might precipitate some action. Margaret had slipped past Hubert to pour herself a cup of coffee and joined the others in the parlour. Antonio greeted Fredrico warmly and learned he had been chosen to make all the arrangements on the trip to England because Fredrico decided he was unable to cope with all the details. And he would have to check with Dr. Mallett for permission to leave the treatment schedule., and Doug added that he and Margaret may have to delay their travel plans as well.

After Margaret had sipped her coffee, she felt a queasiness and said, "I think I may have to leave you now and take myself off to bed because the serum's effects are catching up to me, now, but I will leave you two gentlemen some words of advice, "Drink water to flush out your systems and stay well hydrated for the next two days when we will all have to pay a visit to Ste. Antoine's.

Three days passed before they presented themselves to Dr. Mallett. He thumbed through a sheaf of laboratory reports. "I want a sample of blood from each of you." He pushed a button on his intercom and Margot appeared bearing a tray of syringes and tubes They held out their arms and Doug and Fredrico rolled up their sleeves. After Margot left the room for the laboratory, Dr. Mallett smiled and said, "Now we will talk and you can tell me how each of you has managed over the weekend.". Within a half hour, the telephone rang and Dr. Mallett listened intently and made some notations on a pad of paper. He turned to Fredrico and said, "The technician reports that there is a noticeable drop in your T4 cells since your last test and that is very good news that you are responding to the treatment with the retrovirus serum, and for you Mr. Parker, the news is the same and I am sorry to tell you Mrs. Parker your blood count shows very little response to your T4cells. So I am going to have to rethink the plan for your treatment. The African strain of the virus may be far more complicated than we previously thought, so I will consult with my colleagues on the best course of action for you. Now, Fredrico and Doug, I would like to repeat the treatment you received last Friday."

"Oh God!" Fredrico groaned. "I'm not sure I can go through that again!"

"You must," Dr. Mallett ordered. "It is imperative to stop this virus quickly before it mutates into something else that could damage you with another lesion in the armpit or the neck. With the good results we have achieved with the both of you I will consider treating Jean Paul Claudet before a similar tumour makes a home in his other lung"

"But," Fredrico protested. "Is he strong enough to withstand the vomiting and diarhea?"

Dr. Mallett rested his hands on his knees and rose to his feet. "We will give him an anti-emetic drug because waiting is not an option."

Margaret rose too and said, "If that is possible then I would like those drugs when I have my next treatment." Dr. Mallett smiled and said, "Don't worry, Margaret, I will take very good care of you."

When the telephone rang again, Dr. Mallett listened and excused himself by asking them to return on the morrow.

When they reached the corridor, Fredrico suggested they visit Jean Paul and Margaret reminded him of the hospital's visitor's policy. "So if you don't mind, I would like Douglas and myself to walk home through the Park. I need some quiet time to think about all of this."

Doug put his arm through hers and led her in the direction of the elevator. They crossed the street and entered the park near Hameau Noticing tears in her eyes, Doug led her to a wooden bench near the waterwheel. As she turned to him she said "I hope I didn't seem rude to Hubert and Fredrico, but I just had to get away. I felt exactly the same as when Dr. Green told me I had ovarian cancer." She burst into tears and Doug fumbled in his pocket for a handkerchief. He put his arms around her and held her close. "Margaret, Margaret, dearest. Don't let yourself get upset. Remember God is with us. He's here now and is taking care of us and you, especially. God is greater than a tiny microscopic virus. Forget the lab report and trust God to undertake for you and for me and Fredrico." She lay her head on his shoulder and drew a deep breath. "I know I should be grateful for all that He has done for us, and when I think of that baby at Beyanatha, I should look around at all the patients in Ste. Antoines' who are only a breath away from dying. But what is death?"

Doug laughed, "Death is only the means to an end. A glorious end when we kneel before our Saviour in heaven."

Margaret stood and pulled Doug to his feet. "Come on, darling. Let's walk through this beautiful creation of His handi-work I'm sure heaven is much more glorious than Versailles"

They lingered long in the gardens, their spirits refreshed by the beauty And by mid-afternoon they turned for home to find Hubert and Fredrico enjoying a cup of tea by the fireplace in the kitchen. Solicitous as ever, Fredrico hastened to boil more water and fetched chairs for them to join the conversation about Jean Paul's enthusiastic response to the proposed treatment. Hubert poured fresh tea and said, "I do hope he will be alright because to me, he seems very weak and this treatment might prove too hard on him."

Fredrico shrugged, "We have to trust Dr. Mallett. and Jean Paul is so anxious to leave the hospital and start painting. He said he still has some unfinished canvases in his studio."

Margaret asked, "Where is his studio?"

Hubert replied, "It's on the top floor of the chateau."

Doug asked, "Could we pop over there and have a look? Margaret tells me that it'the chateau is a beautiful place and I'm awfully curious to see it."

"Of course," Fredrico replied. "I like wandering through the place, too. I've always thought it would be interesting to do a film showing the chateau. In a minor way we did when I first met Jean Paul, but then I had no idea it would be such a big story. We'll have to wait until morning though because it will soon be dark and Jean Paul has turned off all the electricity because he said he couldn't afford the bills. I believe him because Paris is known as being a very expensive place to live. Let's celebrate our good health report by going out to dinner in Montparnesse. The prices are reasonable because it caters to the resident artists' community and Jean Paul has a very good friend who owns the Pickled Onion where we can get a good steak."

"Sounds good to me," said Doug."

The Pickled Onion was located on a narrow sloping street at the top of a long hill in a densely populated district in Paris. The sidewalk cafes were full of young people enjoying a pleasant April evening with the ambience of street musicians playing accordions. "We should have called ahead for reservations." Hubert murmured. "We'll be lucky to find a place to park."

"Don't worry," Fredrico murmured. "These poor artists can't afford cars so it shouldn't be a problem."

Pierre Pompier, a portly restaurateur, greeted them effusively, inquiring for Jean Paul and seated them at a table near the open window where Margaret and Doug enjoyed watching the strollers, walking arm in arm, singing La Vie en Rose. The haunting melody remained and when they had returned home after a superb steak dinner, Doug sang to Margaret as they prepared for bed. She said," This has been a perfect evening and I'll never forget it as long as I live." Doug cuddled her closely and added, "which will be a long long time."

During a very late breakfast, Fredrico announced that they would tour the chateau before his meeting with Antonio at lunch. Hubert brought out the keys and they descended the path to the front entrance of the chateau. The glass vestibule was chilly as it was on the north side of the building and quite shaded. Proceeding through the heavy oak door the beauty of the shining white marble foyer burst upon them as the sunshine streamed through the stained glass windows above the staircase. Doug, almost speechless, was reduced to a "Wow!"

"I thought that might be your reaction," Fredrico smiled "Shall we go on upstairs?"

The group followed him up the wide curving steps until they reached a long cool corridor. Tempted to examine what lay behind closed doors. Hubert was relieved to find all the French provincial furniture remained exactly as he remembered it. "No woodworm," he sighed after a careful examination.

Fredrico pushed a door open. "Let's leave the doors of the bedrooms open so the place can be aired out," They continued upwards on another oak staircase with a beautifully carved balustrade and reached another long corridor with many doors. "Here. This is Jean Paul's studio." He walked slowly into the room which faced the north with large windows. The odours of paint and solvent permeated the atmosphere. The room was sparsely furnished with a comfortable chair and a desk with large volumes of art prints on top, and a draped easel stood before the window. "Well, let's see what my friend is working on." He removed the drape and stepped back with a small gasp. The others came to his side to see a remarkable likeness of Fredrico laughing in the sunshine. His tanned complexion emphasized his white teeth and silver hair. "It's St. Tropez," he said "We were there last summer." Hubert viewed the painting thoughtfully. "It's very flattering, Fredrico. I always knew you were a handsome man." Doug clapped his hands. "Were? Hubert? Fredrico still is a handsome man."

Margaret laughed and echoed Doug's sentiments. "I think you are blushing Fredrico, but you can't deny it. You are a very handsome man. I told Douglas you were after we first met. I think he was a little bit jealous, but he's handsome too so it shouldn't matter."

Fredrico shuffled his feet and said, "Now let's see what else Jean Paul has been doing." He lifted several canvases leaning against the wall. "My goodness, more St. Tropez. Here's the main street and the flower market and the café overlooking the marina. The last one is a sunset. I think everyone who comes to St Tropez wants to photograph or paint a sunset but this one is one of his best. Can you believe the blue Mediterranean turns dark green as the light fades.?"

Margaret rubbed her chin "And the sails of the boat have actually become red reflecting the colour of the sky."

Doug began to sing, "Red sails in the sunset far out on the blue, are bringing your lover home safely to you." Fredrico remarked, "You have a wonderful voice, Douglas. Margaret is a fortunate woman to have love songs at her side day and night."

Margaret giggled, "It doesn't take much to set him off. You mentioned day and night. He's liable to break into Cole Porter's song." Doug seized Margaret around the waist and whirled her around singing, "Night and day, you are the one, only you and you alone under the sun." He continued waltzing around the studio, humming aloud until Fredrico, looking at his watch, said, "Sorry to interrupt the fun but I must leave you now, Antonio is waiting for me at the Ritz."

The Ritz?" Doug asked. "Is that near the Louvre or Notre Dame?"

"Within walking distance of both," Fredrico replied.

"Then would you mind if we hitched a ride with you? There's more of Paris we want to see."

"Of course there is." And Hubert can take you to the front door. I hate driving in Paris which sounds strange after driving around in the city of Rome There are just as many reckless Italian drivers as there are French."

With their afternoon plans settled, Margaret said she would like to find a hat if they were going into a church on a Sunday.

Hubert then asked if she was a Catholic and would be seeking the services of a priest and if not, then a scarf would be quite appropriate to wear in the cathedral.

After the men had changed their jackets, the Fiat set off for the centerville and dropped Fredrico off at the revolving doors of the prestigious hotel Ritz across the street from a large shallow concrete pool where little boys were attempting to rig their miniature sailboats. As there was no breeze, the boys took off their shoes, rolled up their pants and waded in pushing the boats and towing them behind them with pieces of string

They came to the cathedral and Hubert questioned them about their itinerary.

Doug patted his guidebook in his pocket. They approached the wide open doors to enter the vestibule and into the long nave with black diamond shaped tiles leading them forward along a center aisle with huge pillars. Wooden chairs were arranged in rows but almost all were unoccupied. A few people sat along the outside walls and Margaret thought they may be awaiting their turn to enter a series of confessionals. Crossing the wide transept they came to the apse where the choir seats were arranged on the high wall beside a huge pipe organ. The main attraction was the glorious rose window, a misnomer, Margaret thought, because the window had three concentric circles of blue stained glass resembling petals. Shades of green and gold were inter changed with the blue, and in the bottom corners were small rose shaped flowers. As the organist began his music, Doug and Margaret walked out of the cathedral with its many statues of unfamiliar saints to the strains of Pax Angelica.

Consulting his guidebook, Doug found the location of the Louvre quite easily because it was such a large building, formerly the palace of the Kings of France and even the Sun King had lived there until he refurbished Versailles. Upon entering the courtyard of the Louvre, they stopped to admire the colossal statues of the Louvre horses.

Before reaching the entrance they entered the pyramids built long ago to exhibit the beauty of the Egyptian empire. The lobby where admission tickets were sold was teeming with visitors. Doug consulted his guide book and rubbed his chin. "This is going to be very complicated," he admitted. "We can never see everything this afternoon. It would take days to see the whole place. What would you like to see, dear?" She looked around and shrugged, "Whatever you want to see is fine with me. But I would like to see the Mona Lisa and the Venus de Milo, and I've heard the Winged Victory is beautiful." Doug smiled and said "That sounds okay and I'll see what I can do."

When he came to the ticket office they were disappointed to learn the Mona Lisa was on tour in China., The ticket agent was sympathetic and so, for a few francs, he directed them to a staircase leading to the upper floors and there at the top stood the Winged Victory's celebration over the centuries of Greece's fight to establish nation hood in a warring world of Rome and the barbarians from the east. On the top floor they finished their search by coming upon the Venus de Milo in her eternal beauty. "She looks like you, darling," Doug said.

Margaret blushed. "My breasts looked like that when I was young, but gravity has taken over now At least I still have my arms. Is she supposed to be Aphrodite the goddess of love?"

Doug smiled and said, "That's her Greek name. The Romans took over the religious system of Greece and renamed all the gods and goddesses. That's why it can be so confusing."

A bell rang signifying the museum was closing and they descended to the lower floor where crowds were exiting through side doors and they found themselves on the Champs Elysee in time to watch the lights come on to illuminate the Arc de Triompe up the street "What should we do now?" Margaret asked. "It's only five-thirty."

Doug stopped walking and said, "I can't believe we have come to Paris and we've never thought of going up the Eiffel Tower! Look, it's just across the river so we'll walk up to the Arc and find a bridge to cross the Seine". A short time later they were seated in a small café, drinking tea and sharing a sandwich. Margaret looked out the window and said, "I always thought the tower would be taller. From here it seems so small."

Doug frowned, "That's odd. It supposed to be one of the tallest structures in the world."

A light shower kept them in the café ordering dessert to keep the waiter happy. When it stopped raining, they left the café, crossing a wide street. Margaret started to laugh, "Oh Doug I was mistaken. Sitting in the restaurant I couldn't see the lower level, but now it seems much larger because it is further away." They descended a long flight of steps to a huge fountain with coloured lights reflecting the statuary and then, down another series of steps to another fountain, and at last they stood gazing upward at the tower with twinkling lights that seemed to reach the stars. Doug bought the tickets for the top level. and they joined the line for the third level elevator. Reaching the viewing platform, Margaret clung to Doug's hand as she felt they were standing in space on the iron grating. Almost as far as they could see, Paris lay before them with lights from the traffic reflecting on the wet pavement. Music from the boats cruising along the Seine. floated upwards on the still moist air. "I think this is almost as beautiful as the night we saw Florence.," Doug said." I'll buy a postcard of this too. I'm sure there's a shop at the entrance."

"What does your guidebook say about the river cruises?" Margaret asked. "I've been wondering how to go home. If the boat stopped near a subway station we could go to Versailles and find our way home from there. I never even thought about what street Jean Paul's house is on or what number it would be if we were to take a taxi".

Doug replied, "I think it's on Rue Chaligny but for the street number I'm lost. I suppose every taxi driver would know where Armand Hammer's chateau is. At least they would know how to get to Versailles. So what would you like to do? The boat cruise and the subway? Or a taxi?"

"The boat cruise sounds more romantic," Margaret replied, "So let's try that."

A crowd had gathered at the boat dock on the bank of the Seine. "I got tickets for a dinner cruise to Versailles," Doug said as he joined

Margaret waiting by a lamp stand. "This way we won't have to handle the subway which might be crowded tonight." The maitre'd' escorted them to a candle lighted table by a large window. Perusing the menu, they decided on a lobster dinner a deux and never regretted their choice. With an orchestra playing dance tunes, Doug said, "Margaret I hope you'll understand if I say that I'm too tired to dance." She reached across the table for his hand. "Of course I understand. We've had quite a busy day and a very busy week. So I love just sitting here and watching the river traffic and the lights of Paris. And oh look! We're passing Notre Dame and there's the rose window illuminated. Isn't it beautiful! Other diners from across the dance floor came to stand beside their table to view the sights and one couple excused themselves for interfering with their meal and returned bringing a magnum of champagne with extra fluted glasses and poured them each a glass of the wine. Much to Margaret's misgivings she raised the glass to her lips and sipped and wrinkling her nose, she smiled at Doug and said, "The bubbles tickle my nose and I warn you, darling. You may have to carry me home." He reached for her glass and said, "I'll drink some of yours. You'll have to make sure I don't become a stumblebum drunk, but at least I hope I can handle this thimblefull. Didn't the apostle Paul tell Timothy to drink only a teaspoon full of wine?"

Margaret narrowed her eyes. "I'm still sober enough to know these wine glasses hold more than a teaspoon. So let's just leave some of it on the table. Now that you have become an international celebrity, you don't want to make the headlines by dropping your tipsy wife in the Seine river in the middle of the night.". He pushed the flute to the centre of the table and said, "Okay, I don't need a hernia to add to our troubles after Dr. Mallett gets through with us next week." She smiled and said, "They're playing La Vie en Rose, let's dance just so slowly with our arms around each other. It's our romantic evening en Pareee."

The boat stopped at a small pier where St Cloud Ave. bridge crossed the Seine. Climbing the steps to the street level, the Parkers saw the spot lights shining on the Palace and knew exactly where they were. With their arms draped around each other they walked slowly along the street and entered Jean Paul's laneway. The light was on beside the front door and Doug pressed the doorbell. Hubert opened the door immediately and with a look of relief he led them into the kitchen to a tea drinking Fredrico.

His warm smile welcomed them as Hubert brought out more cups and saucers. "Hubert was thinking we should go out to look for you."

Margaret laughed, "'Do you send out St. Bernards with a cask of brandy around their necks?"

"No, no," Hubert replied. "They only do that in Switzerland if you're lost in the snow. In France, we wait until bodies show up floating in canals or lying in alleys, stabbed and robbed." Doug loosened his tie and sat at the table. "This has been one of the most memorable nights of my life. We've been up the Eiffel Tower down the Seine on a romantic dinner cruise, drinking champagne, and now, I think Margaret and I should toddle off to bed while we can still climb the stairs. So I'll say goodnight and we'll see you in the morning.." Margaret waved goodbye and said, "Thank both of you for waiting up and looking out for us."

In the privacy of their bedroom when Doug became amorous, Margaret hesitated and said, "I hate to throw cold water on our romantic evening but, darling, we have to be realistic but I'm still infectious to you. Now that you're conquering the one virus, I dare not give you mine, which according to Dr. Mallett is still thriving, so I'm not going to share it with you."

"Okay," Doug mumbled. "I'll behave myself. We've had plenty of romantic evenings so I'm not going to complain. We can always check with the doctor what to do for the rest of our lives."

Monday morning, they presented themselves on the eighth floor of St. Antoine's. Fredrico was anxious to see Jean Paul so they went directly to his room and found him sitting in a comfortable chair in his bath robe. He rose quickly to greet Fredrico with outstretched arms and assured Hubert that he was feeling better than he had for months. Dr. Mallett rose to speak to Doug and Margaret. "Would you like to come along to the office for a brief consultation.?" he asked.

Margaret's stomach churned as she followed him across the hall to sit on a hard wooden chair as the doctor perched on the edge of his desk and glanced at Doug who sat twisting his hands. "I wonder if you are ready to take a chance on a new treatment that may have come our way. I've been in touch with the experts in Africa and the best they have come up with is a new vaccine developed in the labs at the University of Kenya in Nairobi. A professor there, has isolated a virus and developed a vaccine that may be the virus that has infected you, Margaret. Would you be willing to test the serum our lab here is producing from this vaccine?"

Margaret glanced at Doug. "Would you happen to know the name of this professor that did the work?"

Dr. Mallett grinned. "I thought it a coincidence that the professor is a Canadian, a Dr. Dorian Parker. Is there the slightest chance that you may know of her?"

Doug jumped to his feet. "Know her! She's my daughter-in-law! She's married to my son!

Margaret stared at Dr. Mallett with shining eyes, "Of course, I'll test the serum. This is a God thing. When can we start?"

Doug was hugging Margaret and weeping, "Oh, thank, You, God, Thank You."

They hushed their voices as they realized Dr. Mallett was attempting to make arrangements over the telephone. When the excitement had died down, he had summoned Margot who was now drawing more blood samples from each of them and before she left for the laboratory she said that she would return to prepare them for their treatments. Doug coughed and said, "I wasn't aware that I would need any more serum after last week."

Dr. Mallett said, "It's just a precautionary measure, Mr. Parker. After your blood is checked today, I want to be absolutely sure that you aren't habouring any more virus. I'll go and break the news to Fredrico now too." he said as he left the room.

"Poor Fredrico," Margaret murmured. "He won't be too happy about this."

"Poor me," Doug murmured. "I'm not too happy about it either."

Margaret kissed his cheek. "I'm happy that we have such a careful doctor who is going to give us medicine to stop the vomiting."

The Parkers spent the rest of the day in bed receiving intravenous infusions, thumbing through French magazines and a French version of the Readers' Digest. "I wish I could read some of these jokes, "Doug grumbled.

"Save them for when Hubert comes in again," Margaret suggested who was enjoying the fashion magazines. Hubert was busy meeting the needs of Fredrico and Jean Paul who had chosen to undergo therapy at the same time as Fredrico. The anti emetic drugs were proving effective as the clock had ticked nine when Dr. Mallett decided his patients were well enough to go home. He was reluctant to release Jean Paul whose temperature had risen during the day and Fredrico hesitated to say goodbye to his long time lover. Hubert drove a silent Fiat through the foggy streets of Paris. Subdued they entered the quiet house and welcomed a blazing fire and a hot cup of tea.. "Well," Doug said. "I think we can put away our basins, Fredrico, and take ourselves to a nice warm bed. At least that's over. I wonder why Dr. Mallett didn't give us the anti emetics before.". Fredrico warmed his hands by the fiery coals. "He explained it to me, Douglas. It appears you and I were guinea pigs and they wanted to see the reaction that serum had on people. So now they know."

"We should say 'thanks a lot" for telling us." Doug replied. "I'll remember to tell him that tomorrow".

"Tomorrow," Margaret affirmed, "We should get down on our knees and thank him for all he's done for us." She proceeded to tell Fredrico and Hubert the story of Dorian's isolation of the virus that Dr. Mallett was using to treat her. Fredrico listened intently. "One day Victory should do a film on this African side of H I V. It has been done by many film makers but this could have a positive ending."

"We'll find out about it tomorrow," Doug added, when Margaret gets her blood results."

Margaret's blood count showed a remarkable change in her T4cells, and Dr. Mallett jubilantly reported the success of the vaccine to the World Health Organization. "This will revolutionize the picture in Africa for millions. Your daughter- in- law should win the Nobel Prize. You will stay in touch with me during the next few months."

"We are planning to return home to Canada before summer," Margaret said "Doug's daughter is going to be married in June.. But we will certainly see you before we leave. By the way I am assuming we are free to travel to England the end of the week".

Dr. Mallett smiled and wished them "Bon voyage."

Printed in the United States
By Bookmasters

Printed in the United States
By Bookmasters